Nash, Rambler

Nash, Rambler

Frank Sennett

Five Star • Waterville, Maine

This novel is a work of fiction. Names, characters, places and incidents are either the product of the author's imagination, or, if real, used fictitiously.

First Edition
First Printing: February 2003

Published in 2003 in conjunction with Tekno Books and Ed Gorman.

Set in 11 pt. Plantin by Christina S. Huff.

Printed in the United States on permanent paper.

Library of Congress Cataloging-in-Publication Data

Sennett, Frank.
  Nash, rambler / Frank Sennett.
    p. cm.—(Five Star first edition mystery series)
  ISBN 0-7862-5034-8 (hc : alk. paper)
  1. Journalists—Fiction.   2. Los Angeles (Calif.)—Fiction.
  3. Motorcycle gangs—Fiction.   4. Survivalism—Fiction.
  I. Title.   II. Series.
  PS3619.E66 N3 2003
  813'.6—dc21
                                        2002043057

Nash, Rambler

Acknowledgments

Although I once served as a reporting intern at the San Bernardino *Sun*, my experience there was uniformly positive. The characters and events in this novel are products of my imagination, as is the San Bernardino *Ledger*.

But for introducing me to the inner workings of a major metropolitan daily, and for making me feel like part of the family during my brief stay, I would like to thank the very real women and men who made the *Sun* such a fun place to work.

I also must thank Pat Wallace, for her fine editing work on this novel; Ed Gorman, for asking to read it in the first place; Keir Graff and Bill Ott at *Booklist*, for giving me the assignment that brought us all together; and Donald Hamilton, for his professional example and kind encouragement.

I'm also grateful to my wife, Heather, and to my family and friends for supporting my writing endeavors over the years. And I wouldn't have made it this far without the assistance of several fine writing instructors—especially Bill Kittredge, Dick Schwarzlose, and Wayne Seitz.

This book is dedicated to my mother and father, who shared their love of mysteries with me early on. As we all know, once the thriller bug bites you, it never lets loose.

Prologue

Shane Littlefeather's voice came over the answering machine at one minute of two.

"Boss, pick up the goddamn phone."

Even though he was calling a local number, the heavy traffic of San Bernardino's D Street growling mightily in the background made Shane Littlefeather's voice sound far away.

He put his hand over the pay phone receiver and looked back at his double-parked cement truck. This wasn't happening like it was supposed to.

"Goddamn your machine," said Shane Littlefeather. "You say call at two, I call and you're nowhere. You can't duck me, boss. Either I get a full-share cut or I talk to the commission." He wished he could hear if someone was sitting by the machine.

"I'm trying again in a half hour," he said after thirty seconds more, "and if you're not there . . ."

Shane Littlefeather paused, startled by the short beep of the answering machine marking the top of the hour, just as a rifle bullet shattered the glass door and slammed into his chest cavity through the small of his back, releasing a crimson spray out the other side.

The second and third shots propelled Shane Littlefeather's immense frame through the phone booth and into a used-car lot. His left hand tightened on the discon-

9

nected receiver as his body bounced off the grille of a Chevy Impala.

Satisfied with the two reports he had heard before the connection went dead, the man at the other end of the line hit the button to erase the recording and finished his roast beef sandwich.

Chapter One

Nashua Hansen emerged from the shower, toweled off his five-foot, ten-inch frame, and put on his seventy-five-cent outfit: a bright yellow Camel T-shirt, size medium, sent to him after he had called a special number in a cigarette ad; blue corduroy walking shorts handed down to him when his father's spare tire had over-inflated; and a pair of waterlogged tennis shoes he had rescued from Lake Michigan. The shiny blue shoelaces had cost seventy-five cents.

Slicking back his dirty blond hair with his hands, Nash walked down the stairs from the relative comfort of his half of a red brick two-flat into the middle of a sultry Chicago afternoon. Evanston lacked the character to have its own weather, Nash thought as he started his BMW 2002. The city couldn't even claim this shitty day.

As he eased the rusty car onto Sheridan Road, however, Nash imagined he might miss even the stickiest Evanston day after a three-month internship in San Bernardino, where the thick L.A. smog worked its way into every cranny like sweat on a sumo wrestler.

Nash parked on the top level of Northwestern University's lakeside lot and stared at the blue wave crests for a moment before making his way to Fisk Hall for the final meeting with his graduate journalism adviser.

Slant Williams, the William Randolph Hearst Professor

of Urban Journalism, was slouched over the desk in his third-floor office, marking a stack of editing tests with a red pen. A stranger might have thought Slant was dead, what with the pasty glow of the skin on the back of his neck and the arching slump of his body, but Nash knew to look at the hands. Alone in his office, Slant never moved more than his pudgy hands, and he used them only to correct papers, or to turn the pages of a book. In others, streamlined motion could be sleek and poetic; in Slant, it was wholly disquieting.

Nash slammed the door hard behind him, but Slant still raised his head as he always did, in slow jerks like a quizzical turtle. After his eyes opened wide enough to discern the figure in front of him, he ducked down again, concentrating on the tests.

"Do you mind? These are due by three."

"It's three-forty-five, Slant." Nash dropped his book bag onto the scarred typing table next to the professor's desk.

"All the more reason. Sit."

Nash pictured Slant's lips moving like an old campground water pump, rusted red and sucking more air than water. He gave thanks for bad posture.

Nash sat staring at Slant and at the black shade drawn over a fall view of the lake. He had overheard several teaching assistants and lecturers poking fun at his adviser's nickname and mannerisms in the past two years. Slant was too philosophical and old-fashioned for a journalism school bent on churning out broadcast media hacks, they said. He even gave a crap about newspapers for chrissakes. He probably didn't even have cable TV. What he did have was a stellar academic reputation and an office better than the dean's. They couldn't scoff at that, Nash thought.

The professor had picked up his nickname through

twenty-seven years of saying to his students, "What's your slant?" Or, "Nice slant on this piece." Or even, "Get your slanty ass in here." That last bit was infrequently uttered and was, Nash decided, shameless self-parody. So, too, was the "Slant Williams" recently stenciled on the door in place of "Professor Archibald Williams." But what the hell, the guy had earned his shtick.

"You're drooling," Slant said when he sat up straight two hours later.

Nash had dozed off after twenty minutes of trying to see the waves through the blackout curtains and was indeed salivating a bit.

"Disgusting stuff, drool. That's why you'll never see me with a dog."

As Nash refocused his eyes, Slant eased an envelope out of his top desk drawer. "This is it. All you'll need. Names, maps, my phone number. Good luck. See you next quarter."

"Thanks for the inspirational words," Nash said. "And the nap."

"One thing." Slant pointed to the envelope. "Ignore those instructions. I've already given you an A, so you can forget about filing any updates and final reports. You're too much of a hot-shot to need me looking over your shoulder."

"Sounds good, chief."

"How old are you anyway?" Slant asked as he opened his right-hand desk drawer.

"Twenty-three."

"Good enough." Slant handed Nash a Dixie cup decorated with yellow butterflies and pulled a bottle of Black Velvet out of the drawer. "A toast to excellence," Slant said, raising his cup to meet Nash's.

Throwing the shot back in a single gulp, Nash felt a slow,

pleasant burn crawl down his throat. He didn't cough, but he felt his eyes watering.

"Now go get your nose bloody," Slant said, pouring himself another two fingers before re-capping the bottle. "And don't call me unless you're dead or dying."

Nash nodded, but Slant was already back to the editing tests.

Chapter Two

Nash headed west out of Evanston on Golf Road, then drove south on I-94, the Edens Expressway, which merged into the Kennedy to Chicago's Loop. He soon turned southwest onto I-55, the Stevenson, and pulled into the first oasis to grab a hamburger and a scratch-off lottery ticket. He won a free ticket. Then he won another ticket. And another. After six tickets—five trips back to the line of downstaters on their way to see their annual Cubs game—Nash finally lost. The grease rose in his stomach.

As he entered the parking lot, he heard shouts. A man in a hunter-orange cap had won a hundred dollars. Nash tried to concentrate on the positives: Dusk was near and hours of perfect driving time were ahead. No need to get upset, he told himself. Still the grease clawed at his throat.

Nash closed his eyes for a few minutes and listened to Van Morrison. His tape deck was broken, so he had to call up the songs inside his head. In preparation, he had listened to five of his favorite tapes three times each in the last two days. So far, it was working.

As the album spun on inside his mind, Nash flashed onto the Cubs fans from the lottery line. He was reminded of the two tickets he'd ordered for the team's upcoming series against the Dodgers in Los Angeles. A day with Sammy Sosa and Kerry Wood would be a refreshing reminder of home in the middle of La La Land. Nash turned off the music halfway through "Domino" and started the 2002. He had beaten the grease. Triumphantly, he turned onto the entrance ramp.

A motorcycle engulfed in flames stood on the shoulder.

His gut instinct was to hit the gas and scoot past, hoping to Christ the bike wouldn't blow as he did.

But a large man stood in the middle of the ramp, wearing a flaming scarf and waving a blackened helmet. Nash thought about driving at the man to get him out of the way, but decided it would be difficult to spook someone when his clothes were already on fire. Instead, Nash approached the man slowly and rolled down the window, ready to ask him to move.

The man walked up to the car. "Can I grab a lift?" he asked. "I think my chopper is going to blow."

Nash shook his head. The man grabbed hold of the door.

"I'll pay for half the gas," he said.

Nash started to move forward, the man running alongside, until he noticed the cycle's long banana seat curling up in an arc over the gas tank.

"All the gas," Nash said suddenly.

"To where?" The biker licked his lips as he watched droplets of fire splash on the speckled blue tank.

"California."

The man paused, watching the seat begin to ooze over the thin metal. "Yeah. Okay."

The man loped around the front of the 2002 and climbed inside as Nash gunned the car down the ramp. In his rear-view mirror he saw customers at the oasis gas station scramble for cover as the bike tipped over. An instant later, the explosion came so loud it erased the songs in Nash's head.

"My name's Homer," the man said, patting out his scarf on the dashboard. "Mind if I smoke?"

★ ★ ★ ★ ★

The thick smell of burnt wool still filled the BMW three hours later. Nash had almost kicked out the man named Homer at the first exit to Iowa City, when he discovered that most of his money had burned up. But he decided to let Homer ride on, at least until the Van Morrison album restarted inside his head.

"I like to have a smoke on the road, but I've always had a problem lighting a cigarette on the highway," Homer explained. With his long, gray-spackled hair and the profound ruts running across his broad forehead, he looked to be about forty-five.

"Even the really good Zippos blow out before you can get lit. Once you get lit, you can suck a smoke real hard and keep it going against the wind, no problem. But first you've got to get it lit. That's one of the biggest problems of being on the road."

"A problem you had solved."

"Well, yeah." Homer paused. "I was visiting a friend of mine in Moline and he had this grill that he lit up with kind of a propane stick. You push a button and a flame shoots out the tip."

"So you took it?"

"No. He gave it to me. If you've been on the road, you understand these problems. Jack thought it was a great idea. Said he was going to buy another one for the grill and one for his bike, too. And that thing worked great all yesterday. I mean, it stayed lit. Hell, it was doing fine today, too, until that little four-by-four cut me off on the ramp."

"What happened?"

"I was trying to light up before I picked up too much speed. Even that thing would blow out over sixty or so and I wanted to get one going before I hit traffic. Can I bum a cigarette off you?"

"I don't smoke," Nash said. "Why don't you light up some more of your cash?"

"Yeah, well, I'm sorry about that." Homer appeared nervous at the prospect of losing his ride. "I can drive to make up my share. You could sleep all the way."

"I'd sleep better with me driving. I didn't expect anyone to pay for gas on this trip besides me. You just got my hopes up for a minute."

Homer nodded, seemingly eager to change the subject. "Like I was saying, this four-runner cut me off and I got so excited, I dropped the damn lighter down my boot. It melted through and caught the grease on my hog. I pulled right over, but I got so busy putting my foot out, I didn't notice my bike going up behind me. And I don't even have insurance."

Homer leaned forward and rubbed his singed foot through the hole in his boot.

"Where were you headed?" Nash asked.

"I don't really know. I woke up last Saturday in a trailer outside Trenton, New Jersey. The dishes were dirty and the yard was full of tires, just like every other day. So I got on my bike to go get a pack of cigarettes and I ended up here."

"Where next, Springsteen?"

"California sounds about right, I guess." Homer held his hand out the window, trailing charred dollars into the high weeds.

"You got a steady thing going in Chicago?" Homer asked three exits later. "Someone you're already missing, or glad to be running away from?"

"No such luck," Nash said. "Journalism school isn't much of a party zone, and I don't have anything in common with the broadcast babes."

"It's a big city out there. You ever thought about casting your net a bit wider?"

"I've tried building a rapport with the counter girls at video stores and coffee shops, but they're usually on to another job before I'm ready to ask them out," Nash said.

"That sounds like more of a chickening-out problem than a side effect of service-industry turnover."

"It takes me a while to establish my personality."

Homer lit another cigarette. "Hell, you're good-looking enough to ask 'em out after establishing you're not a psycho. And lots of women are even willing to take a flier on psychos, in my experience."

"Yeah, well, I'm not comfortable with the quick-hit approach," Nash said. "They're not in a bar. They're at their jobs."

"How many visits are we talking? Three? Fifteen?"

"Somewhere in there. My best prospect—"

"Maybe you'd have better luck if you stopped thinking about them as prospects . . ."

"My best, what? Chance at scoring? There was this sweet, intelligent knockout who worked evenings at the Blockbuster near my apartment, and I'd go in on weeknights when it was dead, pick two or three great movies—showcasing my exquisite taste—and chat her up for twenty minutes at the counter."

"So what went wrong?"

"Her, I actually asked out. And she seemed into the idea. Only she was moving to Germany in two weeks to get her MBA in international finance."

"How about a fling before she left?"

"I pretty much ruined that possibility when I said, 'I gave up renting porno just to impress you, and now you tell me?' "

"That's pretty funny."

"She didn't think so. Kicked me out of the store. And the next time I came in, they told me she'd quit two weeks early."

"You know who you should try?" Homer asked. "Bank tellers."

"Why?"

"They tend to stay on the job longer than those retail honeys and they're usually looking for a little excitement."

"I don't know if I could flirt with all those cameras watching me," Nash said.

"Well," Homer intoned, "whoever you do go after, at least try to pull the trigger a bit sooner next time."

At a gas station in Iowa, Homer bought the first of several cartons of Marlboros he smoked on the trip. He puffed so incessantly that he used only one book of matches all the way to California.

"Doing my part to cut down on pollution," he said as he lit a new cigarette with the embers of the previous butt.

Homer was a polite smoker, making sure to exhale out the window most of the time. He even asked Nash if the smoke bothered him, seeing as how he hadn't taken up the habit himself, but Nash said the experience would prepare him for the smoke-filled newsrooms he expected to encounter during his career.

"Aren't newspaper reporters out of style these days?"

"Maybe. But I've always wanted to meet powerful people and rake them over the coals. I couldn't pass up that whole watchdog of democracy thing."

"They paying you for this gig?"

"Five hundred a month."

"You must be independently wealthy."

"I've been saving for this trip the past two years." With the fifteen hundred in salary and the thousand he had in the bank, Nash hoped he'd be able to squeak through three months without having to sleep in his car. He'd get a part-time job if he had to.

"You'll probably have to live in some rat hole," Homer said.

"I'll get by."

"Oh yeah, you'll get by. But why get by when you can get it on?"

"What?"

Homer paused. "Well, we're both going to be in California for a while, and neither one of us is exactly a man of means. But I was thinking, if we put what we have into a common pot, we could live in high style."

"Do I look insane to you?"

"Well, no," Homer said, warming to the pitch, "no you don't. We're both rational men, and I think we've been getting along pretty good the last day or so. We haven't argued once, we've got the same taste in music and we both love the adventure of the open road."

"So there you have it?"

"There you have it."

"Am I supposed to float you until you get a job, or are you just going to knock over a liquor store when the rent's due?"

"What kind of a guy do you think I am? I've got plenty of cash sources." Homer actually seemed wounded by Nash's remark. "I'll tell you what. You probably saved my life yesterday, so I'm going to cut you some slack on that back talk. And I'm willing to pay half the expenses."

Slant was always saying that an open mind was more important to good journalism than open eyes, Nash thought, but this guy was destined for serious trouble. Still, the extra cash would allow him to visit Mexico and the coast on his weekends off. And he always liked to enter new places with an ally or two, especially one as big as Homer.

"What if I say no?" Nash asked, finally.

"I'd have to kill you." Homer lit a fresh cigarette and stared at Nash through a haze of smoke.

"If you don't have the rent money by the time we get there, I'll kill you first." Nash threw Homer a steely glance.

"I like your style," Homer said, laughing.

Nash was glad he did.

Chapter Three

The city of San Bernardino sat about five thousand billboards east of Los Angeles, clinging tightly to the San Bernardino Mountains. Beyond that small range, Nash's research indicated, lay the bulk of San Bernardino County, with more square miles than any other county in the Lower Forty-Eight. The outlying desert held the community of Boron (which lent its name to a country-club penitentiary for tax evaders, embezzlers, and fraudulent businessmen), and Edwards Air Force Base, with a dry lake-bed that turned into the world's largest parking lot the night before every space shuttle landing. Route 66 ran through town, as the song says, and there was still a local motel next to the highway with rooms shaped like large teepees.

The city used to be connected to all of this. Until the smog blew into town. On a bad day, or in a bad month, thick clouds of haze plumed up from L.A. and obscured even the mountains from view, as if by some Hollywood special effect. When a freeze threatened the few remaining orange groves in winter, the smudge pots added a local flavor to the smog, giving the residents a perverse sense of pride and ownership.

It was a bad Friday morning when Nash and Homer pulled off I-215 into the northwest corner of San Bernardino, a day in which no one was taking any pride. They pulled into a Denny's and bought a copy of the San Bernardino *Ledger*.

"My eyes like to burn out of my head," Homer said, unwrapping a wet-nap he'd found in the BMW's glove box.

He unfolded the napkin and rubbed it into both eyes as he and Nash walked into the restaurant's waiting area. Just as the lemony scent hit Homer's nose, he felt the searing effects of the wet-nap's chemical coating on his corneas.

"EEEEEEYAHHHH!" Homer said.

The Denny's breakfast crowd paused to stare.

"We'd like a table for two, please," Nash said to a waitress named Wendy as Homer ran for the bathroom.

"Smoking or no?" Wendy asked.

He liked her already. "No smoking."

She pointed to a booth along the far wall. "I'll be over in a minute to take your order."

When Wendy came by the first time, Homer still hadn't returned from the bathroom, so Nash ordered him a stack of buckwheats and a caramel roll. Homer had ordered pancakes and a roll at every meal from Iowa to California. At a two-dollar smorgasbord in Las Vegas, Homer had eaten fourteen full-size pancakes and six butterhorns. Nash hoped Homer's injury would temper his appetite.

Nash was halfway through his first cup of coffee when Wendy stopped by to check on him.

"I don't think that's going to keep you awake," she said. "You look too tired."

He wasn't tired enough to miss the fine strawberry bangs wisping down over her pale blue eyes, or the soft dimple that formed on the left side of her mouth when she smiled.

"My friend and I traded driving shifts straight through from Chicago," he said, slumping his shoulders for effect. Wendy was shaping up to be the highlight of the trip.

"Why were you in such a rush?"

"I'm starting an internship at the *Ledger* on Monday and I wanted to get settled in before my first day."

"Do you have a place lined up?"

"That's the problem. I don't know anybody in town and I didn't want to rent a place before I checked it out."

"What price range are you looking for?"

"Anything cheap as long as it isn't gangbanger turf. Got any advice?"

"If you don't mind a little commute, Redlands is nice." She twisted a loose strand of hair around her finger as she talked. "And over in Shandin Hills by the university isn't too bad. You're working at the *Ledger*, though. It'd be better if you could be close to downtown."

"True enough." Nash wanted to reach out and run his fingers through her hair, too. "So, do you go to school here?"

"I take night classes over at Cal State."

"What are you studying?"

"It's pretty silly."

"I know the California schools have some weird majors, but how bad could it be? Is it macramé?"

"No."

"Zen archery?"

"Wrong again."

"Plate tectonics?"

"Nope." She was laughing gently now.

He leaned in toward her, and was about to introduce himself, when a grizzled hand reached over the back of the next booth and tugged at Wendy's sleeve.

"I've been staring at the bottom of my bottomless cup of coffee," said the cowboy-hatted man attached to the hand. "But I just know you're the gal who can fix me up right."

"That's me," she said, picking the coffee pot off the corner of Nash's table and giving him a wink as she turned away. After pouring the old man a refill, she dispensed a bottle of

25

ketchup from her apron pocket to a family of five at the table across the aisle. And then she was gone, sucked back into the vortex of the breakfast rush.

A few minutes later, just after another harried server dropped off their breakfast, Homer emerged from the bathroom patting at his eyes with a wet paper towel.

"I soaked 'em good but they still sting like hell," he said.

When they pulled out of the Denny's twenty minutes later, Homer was still mad about the wet-nap.

"You could have warned me," he said, working on a theme he had been developing in the restaurant. "You just watched me doing it."

"Hell, it couldn't have bothered you that much; you ate in record time," Nash said, setting up Homer to express theme number two.

"Shut up."

They spent the rest of the morning looking at an ever-more-depressing collection of rundown duplex apartments and by-the-week motel rooms. The first one, which seemed to be furnished exclusively with pieces found by the roadside, featured hot water only in the kitchen, a square of cardboard where the bathroom window used to be and a next-door landlord who expected tenants to help keep her Doberman fed and watered.

Nash looked back on it almost fondly after seeing the last place. Sandwiched between two freeway interchanges on the city's industrial outskirts, it advertised "11th Night Free!" on a ripped plastic banner hanging from the second-floor railing.

"I'd kill myself by day six," Nash said after they toured a particularly dank room where both the phone line and TV cable had been pulled out of the wall. But the twenty-year-old Magnavox was still securely bolted to its metal stand.

"Lunch break?" Homer asked, his appetite forever unflagging.

Nash smiled for the first time in hours. "I know just the place."

The afternoon Denny's crowd was smaller and seemed more laid back than the morning caffeine freaks had been. Nash made sure he and Homer were seated in Wendy's section again, but a server named Dave greeted them instead.

"Chicken-fried steak," Nash said, resolving to drown his disappointment in creamy white sauce.

"I'd stick with the burgers if I were you. That gravy's thicker than motor oil." It was Wendy, looking as fresh-faced as she had four hours earlier. She'd exchanged the apron for a green Windbreaker. "Dave here has eight hours of hell ahead of him. But me, I'm free until dawn."

"Then why are you still here?" Dave asked. "Whenever my hand is clocking out, my feet are already out the door."

"I just saw my new friends here and thought I'd buy them a Coke." She sat down next to Homer, opposite Nash. "Sorry to ditch out on our conversation earlier."

After Dave finished taking their order, Nash introduced Wendy to the biker.

"We met briefly this morning, didn't we?" she asked. "How're those eyes doing?"

"Better now," Homer said. "After watching pretty boy at every meal, it's good to have some eye candy for dessert."

She gave him a sideways smile, then turned to Nash. "I think your friend's hitting on me."

"Settle down, Homer," Nash said.

"That's okay," Wendy said. "I get a lot of that in this job."

"You've got an infectious personality."

"And with my red hair and this jacket, I look like a Christmas tree," she added.

Dave returned with the Cokes and Wendy relaxed back into her seat. "So where were we?"

"What?" Nash asked.

"In our conversation. When I was so rudely torn away this morning."

"I believe you were going to tell me your major." He knew that's where they'd left it. He'd replayed the exchange in his head half a dozen times during the hunt for housing.

"Ah. English. Creative writing. I want to be a great poet." She drew the last word out and grimaced comically.

"What's wrong with that?" Nash asked.

"Everything. No money, no future. I should have picked a more practical career, like you did."

"Hey, I'm embarrassed about my major, too. Sometimes I think I'm the last journalist in America who doesn't want to be on TV."

"We were both born at the wrong time," she said, grinning.

He glanced over at Homer, who raised an eyebrow and gave him a "way to go" nod. Emboldened, Nash said, "We should get together and commiserate sometime while I'm here."

"That sounds nice." She leaned her elbows on the table. "But you do realize I don't even know your name, so it's going to be hard to track you down."

"It's Nash Hansen. And I'd give you my address, but I don't have one yet."

"Right. We were working on finding you an apartment earlier." She paused, as if deciding something. "I've got an idea. Hang on a second."

She walked over to the phone behind the cash register and turned her back to him while she dialed. After Homer and Nash had started in on their patty melts, Wendy slid back into the booth.

Nash pointed at the phone with his fork. "What was that all about?"

"I just called the *Ledger* to see if you're for real."

"You're no poet," Nash said. "You're Bob Woodward."

"You wouldn't believe some of the bullshit stories I hear around here. They keep me on my toes." She took a sip of Coke. "If you need to get into an apartment today, you should really take a look at my building. It's a big complex right near downtown and there's always a vacancy."

"You're kidding."

"Nope. You seem like the sincere type. Call it poetic instinct."

Call it divine intervention, Nash thought.

"This place ought to be perfect for you," she said. "I came down here from Sacramento last year to be near my boyfriend and they let me move in the same day."

Wendy's sly smile told Nash that disappointment had registered on his face the moment she'd said the b-word. She wrote directions to the building on a napkin and promised to give the rental office a call on his behalf.

"This is crazy," Homer said as they approached the group of low-rise buildings. "Gated entrance, volleyball court. No way can we afford this." Homer had called his buddy in Moline, a gregarious pot dealer, and badgered him into wiring out a thousand dollars, but he wanted to make it last a while.

They were greeted in the rental office by a crisp woman in a loose suit with peaked shoulders. She showed them a newish two-bedroom with a small balcony for six-fifty. The sparse furnishings had been assembled out of boxes from Target or Wal-Mart. But the place was reasonably comfortable and clean—a relief after the morning's tenement horror show. The woman agreed to let them rent by the month and Nash wrote out traveler's checks for the first one.

While Nash called to set up phone service, Homer laid out the security deposit in cash, then walked off to apply for a job at a car detailing shop he'd seen a few blocks away.

Early that evening, Wendy stopped by and invited Nash over to her apartment for sandwiches. As he told her about the burning motorcycle, he couldn't help noticing the way her lips moved as she took short sips of milk out of a tall straw. She would bring the glass halfway to her mouth and then lean over slightly to meet the straw, pushing her upper lip over the lower one, as if she planned to take the milk in through her teeth. Nash imagined free straws were probably one of the few perks of working at Denny's. Apparently, Wendy made the most of it. She seemed like the type who made the most of everything.

"If you want to go shopping for house stuff, I can take you to some good thrift stores tomorrow," she said. "But you need to relax tonight. Maybe we could go see a movie."

"Won't your boyfriend mind?" Nash asked.

"Oh, didn't I mention that Bill got transferred to the Philippines?" She was grinning.

"He's in the service?"

"Career Army. But remember, he could be called back at any time."

"Not tonight, I hope."

"Not tonight."

Chapter Four

Trap slices moviegoer's foot
by Nashua Hansen
Ledger Staff Writer

A steel, coil-spring trap set near the snack bar of the Star-Time Drive-in Theater, 20925 W. Ransom, nearly severed the foot of a San Bernardino man Friday night, police say.

Ronald Slasnik, 19, was listed in stable condition at San Bernardino General after the incident, a hospital spokesman said, and surgeons were able to reattach his left foot.

Alerted by the injured man's screams, snack bar attendant Trudy Waylin discovered Slasnik 50 yards from the concession stand entrance about 10:45 P.M. Friday during a showing of *Space Carnival*.

"The teeth had chewed right into his ankle," Waylin said.

Police Lt. Randy Gross said 911 dispatchers received a call from Waylin at 10:53 P.M. and immediately sent an ambulance and three squad cars to the scene.

Officers questioned dozens of moviegoers at the three-screen theater, as well as Star-Time personnel, Gross said. No one was arrested, but the incident is under investigation.

"This was a sick and senseless crime," Gross said. "We are making this a priority case."

No similar incidents have been reported in the county, he said.

Chapter Five

"Pretty good walking in with a story like this on your first day," assistant city editor Lydia Sorenson said as she and Nash went over the piece. It had run in the Sunday Metro section pretty much unchanged. Monday mornings were quiet at the *Ledger* and two reporters had already been kind enough to congratulate Nash on his first effort, modest though it was.

"Jerome Madson, our cops reporter, was asking about you this morning," Sorenson said. "Jerome loves the sick ones. He was only about a mile away from the drive-in last night. Cops pulled a family of three out of a supermarket Dumpster—no visible signs of trauma, just dead. Lot of bad stuff happens in that neighborhood."

News had been far from Nash's mind at the Star-Time as he made his way back to the 2002 with a large popcorn and two Cokes. He was remembering how Wendy had nestled her head against his shoulder during the first feature.

But the moans coming from the poor guy in the trap stopped his daydreaming cold. Nash had tried to pull the claws open, but his hands kept slipping on the slick blood. The snack-bar girl tried to help, but the trap had ground deeply into the bone. Nash held the man's head in his lap and attempted to distract him by asking his name, age, and where he lived and worked. The questions didn't make the man forget his pain, but they did give Nash the basis for a hell of a story.

33

Wendy screamed when he came back to the car covered in blood, but she calmed down considerably when he told her what had happened.

"Wait'll they hear about this at Denny's," she'd said.

Now they were reading about it all over town.

"Is it okay if I turn in more stories I come up with?" Nash asked Lydia Sorenson as she looked toward the large conference room. The editorial staff was filing in to hash out the story lineup for the next day's edition and Lydia was bouncing on the balls of her feet in anticipation. This action, coupled with her diminutive stature and spiky black hair, made her look much younger, and less mature, than her thirty-five-odd years.

"Initiative's fine," she said. "But any assignments we give you come first. And if you can't check in with me before you hit the streets, leave a message in my intranet mailbox. The password is 'tattoo'."

Kathy Carwell, the *Ledger*'s managing editor, was waving the rest of the editorial staff into the glass-walled room. Lydia Sorenson abruptly turned and sprinted to catch news editor Mike Cole before he left the editing bay. Everyone within thirty feet could hear her trying to convince Cole that the latest military base closure story deserved the lead page-one slot as they walked to the conference room.

"We've got photos of them loading stealth bombers on flatbeds with a crane," she said as the features and sports editors passed by. "Color shots. Great stuff. And human interest up the wazoo. Come on, Mike, this is better than a couple of bug-infested citrus groves."

"Base closures are pretty old news by now. And there are still plenty of people who make their living off oranges around here." Cole was warming up. A lifelong resident of San Bernardino, he apparently liked to tweak newcomers like

Lydia. "Besides, what will people be having for breakfast tomorrow? Orange juice or airplane fuel?"

"When the last of those bases close a lot of people around here won't be able to afford breakfast, period."

As the argument continued into the conference room, Nash realized he had been staring at the scene quite stupidly, drinking in his first day as a member of the working press.

"She's got a tongue on her like to whip your eyebrows off if you get too close." It was Curt Escobar, the *Ledger*'s political reporter. Nash had met him briefly on his inaugural tour of the newsroom.

Although he couldn't be described as fat, Escobar was not a candidate for fitted dress shirts. He had a lean face and his rolled-up shirt sleeves revealed muscular forearms, but he had sprouted a fair-sized pair of love handles somewhere along the road to middle age. These he kept covered with a brown corduroy jacket, which had seen its best days sometime during the first Bush administration. The mustache was vintage seventies. A new pair of cotton Dockers and a close-cropped haircut were all that saved Escobar from looking completely behind the times.

He said, "My advice to you is, stay way over on Lydia's good side. If you give her a bone to chew and she finds any nasty splinters, you're history."

"How's that?"

Escobar snared Nash's cuff and led him to his cubicle overlooking the street. Campaign buttons, hotel napkins and reporter's notebooks were tacked and strewn everywhere. Most of the other cubes were decorated with plants, a few family pictures. But Escobar's was as cluttered as a transient's shopping cart.

Escobar pulled half a Twinkie out from under a silk tie and

shoved it into his mouth as he pulled out a chair for Nash.

"We had an intern here maybe two years ago. Northwestern guy like yourself. He's doing just fine for about a week and a half, then he goes out to cover some speech. Visiting dignitary bullshit, something. Anyway, they're serving cocktails—it's down at the Moose Lodge and all the Moose are having a traditional liquid lunch. Well, our boy tucks into a couple of drinks himself, comes back, writes the story no problem. Except there is a problem."

Escobar pulled his chair closer. His voice was so conspiratorial that Nash had to fight the urge to look over his shoulder to check on Lydia. The impulse was strengthened by the smear of errant Twinkie filling that Nash could now see in frightening detail on Escobar's lower lip. Still, Nash maintained eye contact.

"Actually there are two problems," Escobar said. "First, Lydia asked a friend, a reporter covering the meeting for the Riverside paper, to watch out for this guy, see how he conducts himself. And second, this kid makes the dumbest mistake you can make. He writes that the speech was at the Elk's Club.

"Okay. Now Lydia gets a call from her friend as this intern is writing the story. I'm hanging around waiting on an interview and I see she's turning around and looking at this kid funny. When he turns in the story about a half-hour later, she takes it from him real cold, right? And when she's done reading it, she calls him into one of those glass meeting rooms and chews him up, man. You can't hear anything, but this pantomime theater is so intense, half the newsroom is watching by the time Lydia's done with this guy. And that was it."

"It?" Nash asked, turning slightly to watch Lydia argue a point in the story meeting, hands flailing.

"Yeah. It. We never saw him again. He just sort of skulked off. So I wanted to tell you, watch your shit."

"Thanks for the warning."

"No problema. Anything else I can tell you?"

"About Lydia? One thing, I guess. Why is her computer password 'tattoo'?"

"Think about it a minute. 'Lydia, oh Lydia, say have you met Lydia, Lydia the tattooed lady'?"

Nash shook his head.

"The Marx Brothers, man. It's a song. I gave her that nickname when she started here five years ago. I know she hates it, but she's been a pretty good sport about it. I'll let you know when I come up with your nickname. If you last that long."

Chapter Six

After his talk with Escobar, Nash walked across the aisle and up to his cubicle next to the education reporter's desk. She was off covering an executive session of the county school board, and, with the editorial meeting dragging on, Nash had the northern end of the newsroom to himself. He leaned back in his chair and read Jerome Madson's story about the dead family.

Sorenson was right: The bodies were discovered near the drive-in. The only paint jobs the houses in that neighborhood had seen in recent years were from the spray cans of gang members. The dead family, a man and woman with their young daughter, was found in the Dumpster of a Von's super-market by the assistant manager of the produce department. Preliminary reports indicated they had been dead less than twenty-four hours. No visible signs of trauma. With one person, it could be a heart attack or stroke. But when an entire family checked out like that, Madson's police sources speculated, it likely meant poison or asphyxiation. They were all wearing their Sunday best.

Who would kill a family on their way to or from church? Nash wondered. He'd heard of families dying of carbon monoxide poisoning from faulty furnaces, but those bodies were always found in their beds.

To get away from such grisly questions, he walked the length of the newsroom to the features department. His trip to the movies had given him an idea for a lifestyle piece and he wanted to pitch it to Faye Krashenko, the features editor.

"So you're the new kid," she said. "I read your gruesome first effort. What do you want with us softies over in features? Looking to write some puff pieces on ax murderers and serial killers? 'Fashion on the run: Four killers give knockout tips'." Faye smiled up at Nash from her editing screen. She was playing with headline sizes for an upcoming fashion supplement.

"Aren't they keeping you busy enough over in the hard news gulag?" she asked as she swiveled out from behind her desk, stood up and gently smoothed the lines out of her clingy blue dress. "Because if they're not, I've got about a dozen good ideas that don't have a writer to go with them. Newsroom layoffs might not be good for readers, but they do open up lots of opportunities for eager interns."

"That'd be great, especially when I start editing copy in a few weeks," Nash said. "Then I don't start until four and I could write for you during the day."

"Fair enough. So what's up?"

"At the drive-in Friday night, before I waded into the blood and guts, I noticed something odd about the place—the whole theater seemed brand-new. It just didn't feel like a drive-in, you know?"

"You mean no used rubbers and broken beer bottles?"

"Exactly. The playground equipment in front of the screen was gleaming under the lights. The snack bar was all velvet ropes and polished brass. And no chipped speakers; just perfect FM stereo sound."

Faye Krashenko nodded. Her long brown hair bobbed against her shoulders. "Sounds like someone's rescuing open-air theaters from extinction."

"Interested?"

"Now that you mention it, I did hear that one of our titans of real estate was buying a few drive-ins a while back. I don't recall the name, but someone in the business department will."

"Is that a yes?"

"It's a good angle. We don't have any historic architecture down here, except for a few Spanish missions. So now there's a big push to save and restore all the kitschy gas stations, theaters, and greasy spoons from the fifties. If this guy spiffed up a couple of drive-ins in a period kind of way, people around here will eat it up."

"I'll get right on it."

"Can you put something together by next Monday? I'd like to run this the following Sunday. I'll assign the photos."

"No problem." Nash extended his hand to Faye Krashenko and immediately felt foolish for making such an awkward gesture. But the features editor gripped his hand without pause. Her long fingers were warm from the computer keyboard and Nash felt a slight shiver as the tips of his fingers glanced off the cool silver of her bracelet.

The business reporter Nash talked to had written about the drive-in acquisitions, but he didn't remember much more than the buyer's name: Evan Carr, an influential real estate speculator who had been making regular appearances in the business pages since the late fifties. The reporter didn't recall when the stories had run, but he did show Nash how to search the *Ledger*'s internal database.

Evan Carr's investment group, CarrCorp., had purchased three drive-ins in San Bernardino two years earlier from movie chains looking to dump their single-screen properties, the story said. None of the theaters were located in central business zones; two were in neighborhoods and one, the Star-Time, was near a group of factories on the outskirts of town. In a brief interview, Carr had said he intended to refurbish the theaters and make them profitable.

"Everyone in Southern California expands into the entertainment business at some point," he'd said. "Fond memories of youth and some positive demographic research led me to choose drive-in theaters."

The accompanying color photo, the main art on the business page that day, showed a smug Carr standing in front of a movie projector with his arms folded across his chest. He looked to be in his sixties, with thinning gray hair, brown eyes, and deep frown lines around his mouth. A standard Brooks Brothers pinstripe jacket was draped over a chair in the photo's left foreground. Nash could see why Carr had wanted to pose in his shirtsleeves. He had the muscles of a man who enjoyed doing one-arm pushups.

Nash printed out the story and returned to his cubicle to arrange an interview. He called the company's general office number and was told Evan Carr was out inspecting a property. Nash described the story to the secretary and left his number.

As Nash was jotting down questions for Carr, Lydia Sorenson tapped on his shoulder.

"Word is you've already started farming yourself out."

He looked up at her. "I got a feature idea last night and I just ran it by Faye."

"Tell you what, Nash. Like I said, I don't mind you showing some initiative, but we've got to have a code of conduct between us. I thought I told you assigned stories come first."

"I'm sorry if I made a wrong move. I didn't think I had any assignments pending today."

"That's why I want you to check in with me first before you pitch story ideas to anyone else. We're short-handed on the news side and your idea might have fit in the local section. Besides, there's an important event I wanted you to cover today. But since you're already tied up . . ."

"Hey, this feature can wait." He closed his notebook. "What do you want me to cover?" He wanted to stand up so he wouldn't feel at such a disadvantage in the conversation, but Lydia Sorenson was so close her toes were touching the wheels of his chair.

"Here's the press release. I know you'll do a good job for me," she said. "Have the story on my desk by six, okay?"

Nash pulled the mimeographed letter out of the torn envelope. It was an invitation to the opening of a new playground near downtown.

"I'll do my best, Lydia." He suppressed a grimace.

"I know you will, Nash."

Chapter Seven

After checking out with Lydia for lunch, Nash drove to the Star-Time to prep for the Evan Carr interview. The neighborhood leading into the industrial zone was less foreboding, but somehow more depressing, in the harsh midday sun. Every store window sported metal security gates. Pudgy children in droopy diapers ran across litter-strewn lawns.

Nash entered the wrong driveway to the theater and had to turn around to avoid a row of metal teeth embedded in the road. A sign warned of "Severe tire damage." Cars could leave the theater over the teeth, but anyone looking to sneak in would pay the cost of four radials in admission. He turned the BMW into the curving entrance and parked in front of a metal gate that extended from the ticket booth to a concrete wall on the far side of the road. The place looked deserted.

As Nash stood at the gate, he saw a man carrying an over-stuffed trash bag in each hand rounding the corner of the squat snack bar about fifty yards away. He waved to the man, who responded with a curt nod.

Thinking the worker might offer some perspective on Carr's operation, Nash sidestepped the gate and arrived at the snack bar just as the man heaved the bags into the Dumpster next to the building. Even though he appeared to be in excellent shape, the man grunted as he hefted each bag. Cups and popcorn boxes must be heavier than he remembered,

Nash thought as he pulled his notebook and pen out of a back pocket.

"Afternoon," Nash said, backing up a few steps as the rank smell from the Dumpster assailed his nose. "I'm here to do a story on your theater for the *Ledger*."

"You got an appointment?" The man pulled heavy work gloves off two gigantic hands and fixed a level stare on Nash's forehead.

"No. I just noticed that the whole theater seems brand-new and I thought our readers would like to know about it." Nash tried to catch the man's eyes, but he continued to stare away as if he lived in a world separate from the one he and Nash were standing in.

"I could call the police on you for trespassing." The man tucked the gloves into his back pocket and briefly lowered his gaze. His left pupil was gray and turned slightly askew; the right one was a troubled green.

"I thought you nodded at me to come in a minute ago," Nash said.

The man squinted. "What do you think I am?" he asked. "A bobble-head doll?"

"I'm not here to write anything negative," Nash said. "I want to do a feature on how your boss is saving drive-in theaters. It'll probably increase your attendance."

"Evan Carr ain't my boss. He might own this place, but I run things 'round here with no guff. Now get the hell out."

Nash nodded slowly and took two steps backward. "Listen, I didn't mean to offend you. I can see that you're running the show here. I'm going to interview Evan Carr, but I thought it would be good to take another look around the place."

"You think you're real smart, hey? You think I don't know what you're up to? Snooping around here. You got nothing

44

on me. Did Carr send you? He's a fool if he did. I ain't broke no laws. I'm protected by the Constitution. You know about that, hey?"

The man lunged forward and clamped his hand onto Nash's left wrist with a grip so tight it made his fingers go limp. Nash watched his notebook fall to the ground.

"I'm just here from the paper," he said. It felt like his wrist bones were being rubbed together. His forearm was numb. "I'm not here to hassle you, I swear. Nobody sent me." Nash felt his wrist crack under the increased pressure. The pain forced him to his knees. As he leaned forward, the man kicked hard into his rib cage. Nash saw black spots on the edge of his vision as the man let go of his wrist and kicked him again, this time in the neck.

"You bring that message to Evan Carr, hey? I'm sick up to here with his crap, you hear?"

But Nash was well beyond hearing. The black spots had eaten his eyes and hot flashes enveloped his consciousness. He barely felt the final kick to his abdomen that rocked him backward onto a gravel speed bump.

Nash heard Van Morrison playing gently to the throbbing beat inside his head. But the music faded as he jerked awake at the sound of a passing fire engine. He felt a tickle in his ear from the vomit that had pooled up under his head. His chest was on fire and when he opened his eyes, he was surprised to find it was still light out. It was the same jarring sensation he had whenever he went to see a matinee and emerged from the soothing escape of the movie into the stark reality of the afternoon light. Nash closed his eyes and rolled slowly away from the vomit, sending jolts of pain up his arm from his shattered wrist as he did. His breath came in heaving bursts and a pinched nerve in his neck made him dizzy.

After a long pause, Nash pushed himself into a sitting position with his good hand and re-opened his eyes. He was behind a large, squat brick building. He looked at his watch; the playground opening was scheduled to start in forty-five minutes.

When he stood up, he vomited again. After wiping his mouth with an old newspaper, Nash walked around the side of the building into a large parking lot. The building was a strip shopping center dominated by a Von's supermarket. He walked the length of the sidewalk and entered an empty Laundromat with a bathroom in the back. He washed his face and hair with a green soap cake and inspected his reflection in the steel cover of the paper-towel dispenser. Aside from the purple welt on his neck and the bruising on his wrist, there was little noticeable damage.

The checkout clerk at Von's gave him directions back to the drive-in. It was about a mile away, she said, and if he stood on the corner, a bus would be along shortly to take him there. As he waited, he wrapped his wrist with white first-aid tape and washed down five extra-strength Tylenol with a Coke. His breathing was coming easier now; it didn't feel like he had any broken ribs.

As the bus carried him toward the theater, Nash tried to piece together the significance of what had happened. The manager of the Star-Time obviously didn't get along well with his boss. Could he be the one who'd set the bear trap? He was mean enough. But why did he think Evan Carr was sending people over to harass him? Maybe the man was just plain crazy and had made Nash a bit player in his hellish delusion. And what had he said about being protected by the Constitution? None of it added up. Maybe it would when he found out more about Evan Carr.

Nash looked up just in time to see the drive-in pass by the bus window. He yanked the cord, forgetting about his wrist, and barely suppressed a scream as the bones grated together like chunks of glass.

Walking back to the Star-Time, Nash kept a close lookout for the large man. He walked up the curving driveway slowly, pressing his back against the concrete wall. His car was still there. Nash loped from the wall to the back of the 2002 and crouched low. He fished the keys out of his left pocket with his right hand and looked through the windshield for signs of life on the theater grounds.

He surveyed the area once more through the glass, then rounded the car and opened the door. As Nash started the engine and shifted into reverse, the man stepped out from behind the snack bar. Nash could feel the stare as he slammed the BMW into reverse and backed around the corner and out of sight.

Chapter Eight

The playground opening was an exercise straight out of news writing class. Nash jotted the names of the speakers in the small notebook he had purchased at Von's and took down a few quotes from the mayor and a spokesperson from a nearby community center. He then interviewed a five-year-old girl and her twin brother about the joys of the teeter-totter.

Nash arrived back at the *Ledger* at four-thirty and had the story finished by five. The sleeves of his dress shirt were rolled down to cover the tape on his wrist, but it was throbbing too hard to allow him to button the cuff.

"Not bad," Lydia Sorenson said when she finished reading the piece. "But what's wrong with your neck?"

"I fell off the monkey bars."

"Still just a boy at heart, huh?" She laughed as if she had made a particularly funny joke. "Well, get out of here and go lie down with a warm rag on it or take a hot shower. The swelling ought to go down by tomorrow."

"Thanks."

"By the way, you got a message to call Mr. Evan Carr. I was going to give it to you earlier, but I didn't want to interrupt great journalism in the making."

Nash felt a sharp throb in his neck, but he managed to smile.

"What's this about? Carr's a pretty big deal in this town."

"Just a puff piece for features, Lydia. Nothing really newsworthy."

★ ★ ★ ★ ★

At the emergency room of San Bernardino County Hospital, a resident chastised Nash for taping up his wrist instead of coming right in. It was fractured, the resident said. If Nash had continued treating himself, he might have ended up needing surgery.

After having been pushed aside by the paramedics at the drive-in Friday night, he was beginning to think that members of the local medical community had some kind of chip on their shoulders. But when the nurse cut off the tape, Nash knew the doctor had legitimate concerns. In the few hours since he had been pummeled by the theater manager, the skin around his wrist had turned a blotchy purple and black. It looked and felt like an overripe banana. When the resident applied pressure to reset the bones, Nash nearly fainted, despite the pain-killing shot he'd been given.

The bad news was that he would have to wear a cast for nine weeks. Fortunately, his Northwestern medical insurance would cover the expense. Since the cast was too big to hide under a shirt sleeve, Nash decided he would have to come up with a story for Lydia. He certainly wasn't going to let her screw up his story.

It would be best to tell her he had fallen down in the shower or tripped on some stairs, he thought as he drove to his apartment. Then he would be free to track down the connection between the drive-in manager, the trap, and Evan Carr. There was no sense pressing charges against the manager. He'd just claim Nash had been trespassing, and probably come gunning for him, too. It would be better to proceed with the feature angle and interview Carr, get a sense of the man and what he was capable of doing.

As Nash pulled into the apartment complex, he noticed about twenty motorcycles parked on the street. He punched in the gate code and parked in a space beneath his balcony. Hard rock music blared from the open door and he saw Homer helping three men in worn leather jackets tap a thirty-gallon keg.

The Doors' "L.A. Woman" hit Nash with the force of a depth charge as he rounded the stairs to the third floor. He swam through waves of sound to his door, which was propped against the wall across from the apartment, plaster-encrusted screws hanging from its hinges. Through the entrance, Nash saw a biker take a huge hit from a bong made out of a ceramic skull and the tail pipe of a Harley hog. In the far corner, another biker had his hands up the T-shirts of two young women with long, stringy hair. About twenty other leather-clad behemoths milled about, drinking, smoking, and grunting to the music. Nash pushed his way through the bodies and walked down the hall to his room. Someone had spray-painted a skull and crossbones and "Keep Out" on the closed door. He envisioned a biker orgy inside, with his clothes being used for sweat rags.

"Hey Nash!" Homer yelled over the music as he bounded down the hall.

"What the fuck!" Nash yelled back, stopping Homer just as he was about to put him in a head lock.

Homer opened the door to Nash's empty room and pushed him inside.

"Check out this party, man," Homer said as Nash looked around his room for signs of damage. "What a day. I got a job detailing cars and then I hooked up with the goddamn Berdoo Angels! These guys are legendary, man. I'm glad my chopper blew up."

"You're going to get us kicked out. Or killed."

"Chill, Nash. I kept them out of your room, didn't I? It's

under control. We're just warming up here, anyways. When that keg is drained, we're going to hit the bars."

"Hell of a cocktail party, asshole."

"Don't worry, man. I'll pay for the damage. Just relax. Have a beer. Maybe you can bring Wendy on over, lower her inhibitions."

"Screw you."

"Hey, she looked kinda wild to me. Anyways, I'll catch up with you later."

Nash followed Homer back into the party. The Angels were older than he would have imagined. Most of them looked to be pushing fifty. Too old to rock 'n' roll, too mean to die, he thought as he watched a fat, balding Angel cut his face, playing with a butterfly knife.

Nash pushed through to the doorway and headed down the hall to Wendy's apartment. As he knocked on the door, he saw a pair of policemen come out of the stairwell.

"I never should have taken pity on you," Wendy said as she took his hand and led him inside. "What's with the cast?"

"Long story," he said. "I'm sorry about all the noise. I guess Homer found himself some new friends." Suddenly, Nash's voice seemed much too loud for the room.

"Hey, the music stopped," Wendy said. "Just in time for dinner. Come on and sit down. Tell me your story." She gave him a hug and grinned up at him. Her hands were soft against the tense muscles of his back. She pulled his head down and gave him a short kiss, then let go and sprinted into the kitchen. It had been a day full of surprises.

"I made lasagna," she said. "Come help me serve it."

Chapter Nine

For the second time in less than twenty-four hours, Nash found himself waking up in a strange place. Leaning over Wendy's pillow to smell the remnants of her perfume, he decided there was no comparison between coming gently out of a deep sleep to the sound of her shower and regaining consciousness in a supermarket trash heap.

The bedside clock read seven-forty-five. Nash didn't have to be at the paper until ten. He began settling in for an extra hour's sleep on the soft mattress when Wendy started to sing "Good Day Sunshine" as she lingered under the water. Feeling a sudden urge to be clean, Nash threw off the covers and headed for the bathroom.

Later, at breakfast, he sat wrapped in a fluffy white towel, watching her leg muscles stretch as she reached for a box of corn flakes on the top cupboard shelf. As she raised her arm, the bottom of her red kimono danced on the tops of her thighs.

"That wasn't bad for a guy who just went fifteen rounds with the Incredible Hulk." She sat down and poured them each a bowl of cereal to go with the blueberry muffins he had heated in the microwave.

"I'd have to have a lot more than a broken wrist to stay away from you after last night."

"I did have a lot of pent-up energy, didn't I?" She touched

the fingernails of Nash's good hand. "I hope you don't think I'm too easy."

"I don't, but I'm not so sure about Bill."

"Bill's been gone for three months now. I think he's decided he loves the Army more than he loves me."

"Bad choice. How many years have you been together?"

She moved her hand away from Nash's and held up five fingers.

"Long time." He began to peel the paper off a muffin.

"It was just one of those high-school relationships that keeps chugging along after graduation because there's never a good reason to end it," she said. "Maybe now there is."

Her devilish grin was back. Nash had to admit he liked it, but it wasn't going to keep him from getting answers to a few nagging questions. "It doesn't sound like you're too upset about the way things turned out," he said. The paper was really sticking to the grooves of the muffin.

"I look at it like maybe Bill thought we both deserved something better than just going along by default."

He stopped peeling when she got up and hugged him from behind.

"I think he was probably right," she said, leaning down to kiss his cheek.

After Wendy made sure the hall was empty, Nash sprinted down to his apartment wrapped in the towel and carrying his grungy clothes. The door was still off its hinges and the living room was filled with the smells of a fraternity house on Sunday morning—stale beer, sweat, and dope. Homer was most likely in jail or at work with a gargantuan hangover, Nash thought as he dressed in the untouched sanctuary of his room. There would be no pity either way. Homer would have to be the one to clean the place up and deal with the landlord.

Nash dialed CarrCorp. and was pleased to get a live receptionist without having to press any additional buttons. She rang him right through to Evan Carr, as if he'd been expecting the call.

"Mr. Hansen, it's a pleasure to speak with you." Carr sounded as if he were talking on a speaker phone.

"Please pick up your receiver, Mr. Carr," Nash said pleasantly. "I believe we have a private matter to discuss."

"I heard about the unfortunate incident at the StarTime," Carr said after a brief pause. His voice sounded much closer.

"The manager seemed upset by my presence." Nash wondered exactly what the man had told Carr about the confrontation.

"I'm very sorry about what happened; it was a horrible misunderstanding. You see, Mr. Snipes is the son of an old friend of mine. He was emotionally traumatized during the Vietnam conflict, and I've employed him through the years as a favor to his father. Perhaps you can understand why he couldn't work for anyone who wasn't sensitive to his volatile condition."

"Post-traumatic stress disorder?" If Carr was helping out Snipes, the manager didn't seem to appreciate the assist.

"Yes, exactly. But Malcolm has done quite well in therapy over the last ten years or so. As a matter of fact, his scuffle with you was his first physically violent episode since the late 1980s. I think you just startled him."

"I wasn't sneaking around, if that's what you mean." Carr's soothing manner had probably served him well in selling condos to retirees, Nash thought, but it wasn't going to make him apologize for taking an unprovoked beating.

"I didn't mean to imply any wrongdoing on your part, Mr. Hansen." Carr's voice was even more mellow than before. "I just know that Malcolm is exceedingly jumpy. Of course, CarrCorp. will pay any medical expenses you incurred in the incident. And I'd like you to join me for lunch this afternoon. We can discuss the story you're working on, if you still want to write anything about my company after what has transpired."

"That sounds altogether civilized, Mr. Carr. I want to do a feature on the restoration of CarrCorp.'s drive-in properties and I'd be a heel to cancel it just because you take care of your friends."

"I'm glad you see it that way, Mr. Hansen. Shall I have my driver pick you up in front of the *Ledger* at twelve-thirty?"

"As long as I can bring along a photographer and you promise to give me a lot of good quotes."

"It's a deal," Carr said with the smoothness of a man telling his favorite anecdote for the thousandth time.

At twelve-twenty-five, Nash spotted a chauffeur doffing his cap to the paper's receptionist at the far end of the newsroom. It was lucky Lydia was still at lunch, he thought as he headed toward the main entrance and waved to the driver. But Nash was sure he'd have some explaining to do when he got back.

He introduced himself to the driver, and then watched the photographer assigned to the drive-in story, a short man in his fifties with a fringe of brown hair wrapped around the crown of his skull, rattle up to the reception desk.

A shooter in the finest sense of the word, Carl Barns was probably the only man in the world who didn't look like a clown in a Banana Republic photographer's vest. Six cameras and several zoom lenses, the largest of which could easily have found a place on the head of a Paris runway model, hung from the vest's various epaulets and loops. Completing the picture was a black, telescoping tripod slung across Carl's back like a bazooka and held in place by a bandolier strap bristling with a good thirty rolls of film.

"Let's get at 'em, Sidney," Carl said to the chauffeur, a slight man with such decorum that he looked upon the mercenary shooter as if he were a head of state.

"This way, sirs," he said, pointing to the silver stretch idling next to the row of news boxes out front.

As Barns clicked and whirred around the CarrCorp. atrium, Nash lobbed powder-puff questions about the drive-in at Evan Carr. Answering in skillful sound bites, Carr nibbled at the corners of a tea biscuit and glanced now and then at a stack of memos on his lap.

The first thing Nash noticed about Carr was that he had added a small paunch in the two years since he'd posed for the photo in front of the projector. The arrogance was still there in his face, but the hair was thinner and the skin had begun to fall slack under his chin. Evan Carr was starting to let himself go, and Nash was curious to find out why.

Even though he was recording the interview on a microcassette placed on the long bench to catch every nuance of Carr's speech, Nash jotted ancillary notes in his notebook. Focusing at first on the plants of the atrium and then on Carr's conservative attire, Nash gradually edged closer to his subject and began reading the memos upside down and scribbling down the gist of them as he asked more questions.

10 wk. dlay on twnhse opning, he wrote. Then, *call mr. harvey, re: auction of hdsn's bay orgnls.*

"Very good, Mr. Hansen," Carr said, leaning over and stopping Nash in mid-question. "That trick has served me well in countless real estate closings."

"I apologize," Nash said, closing his notebook abruptly. "I

guess I'm as indiscriminate as a vacuum cleaner when it comes to sucking up information."

"No blood, no foul." A noise halfway between a chuckle and a growl came from deep in Carr's throat. "As a matter of fact, I'm holding you in higher regard with each passing moment. Nice how you turned off the recorder as soon as you realized I'd caught you peeking, for instance."

"Have I overstayed my welcome?" Nash asked as he pocketed the tape machine.

"Not at all. This type of sport is good for the blood. You're understandably still on guard over yesterday's incident, which means you're not a fool. So why not dispense with the foolish questions and tell me what you've really come to find out?"

"Let's start with the bear-trap incident last Friday. Any connection between that and your deranged manager?"

"Off the record?"

"Sure. This isn't part of my assignment."

"Well then, yes, we do believe there is some connection to poor Malcolm. But this mustn't see print. I have promised to protect him always."

"What do you have besides suspicions?"

"For one thing, the trap was taken from my collection. It's mostly beaver strings, but I have a few bear traps as well. And Malcolm was the only CarrCorp. employee at the drive-in that night who has been to my private display room. As I've said, Malcolm's father is a close friend, and I have them both over for dinner regularly. Malcolm often looks over the collection while his father and I converse."

"Have you discussed the matter with the police?"

"Regrettably, no. And by fulfilling my duty to protect Malcolm, I fear I've forever lost a fine piece of work."

"Which cut up a fine piece of a man's foot."

"Would knowing who set the trap take the scars away?"

"No. But a court settlement could buy some awfully nice crutches."

"Check up on the matter if you wish, but I give you my word that CarrCorp. is assuming liability in this matter and has offered a considerable sum to the man and his family. As you see, my motives are pure."

"You want to see what old Malcolm will come up with next?"

Carr shook his head slowly. "We are looking into some rather specialized counseling. The decision is best left to the family."

"So to reward yourself for these kind deeds, you're planning to pick up a few more traps from the famous Hudson's Bay Company."

"Traps are a natural extension of my passion for making a quick, clean killing in real estate." There was that animal noise from Carr's throat again. "But I become just another compassionate family man when I leave the office at the end of the day."

I suppose that's why you display the traps in your house, Nash thought.

"It has been a distinct pleasure talking with you, Mr. Hansen." Carr stood and directed a smile somewhere behind Nash. "My assistant is waiting beyond the waterfall to show you and Mr. Barns out."

Nash had forgotten about Carl; he had just seemed to disappear into the foliage. But once inside the limo, the photographer broke into a conspiratorial grin.

"I overheard your little tête-à-tête from behind the hydrangeas," he whispered. "That guy's gonna eat your balls for lunch."

"You don't think I can handle myself?" Nash asked.

"Maybe you're spending too much time looking through your viewfinder to know up-and-coming talent when you see it."

Barns laughed. "It doesn't necessarily matter how good you are when you're the new mouse and an old snake like that catches your scent."

"Maybe so," Nash said, eager to change the subject. "Speaking of old, why are you still lugging that ancient hardware around anyway? I thought all the pro shooters were going digital."

Barns looked down at the array of photographic equipment hanging from his vest like talismans. "For one thing, the *Ledger* is too cheap to spring for top-of-the-line digital cameras," he said. "The ones they'd buy have such low pixel counts that most of the shots come out muddier than a riverbank in spring. Plus, I've been shooting with rigs like these for thirty years. I know all their tricks, and I don't feel like learning any new ones."

"You've been in this game a long time," Nash said.

"Long enough to smell trouble," Barns replied. "If you need any more help with the Carr situation, just ask."

Chapter Ten

Nash ate his lunch in the *Ledger*'s morgue, hoping to avoid Lydia and get some grunt work done on the Carr investigation. He reread the drive-in story and found the name of the general contractor on all three jobs, Warren Construction of Rancho Cucamonga. Then he pulled out the construction file and looked for references to Warren.

Apparently the company was not a major player in the local construction community; it had been mentioned in only three stories over the past five years. The first one was an overview of recent building activity in the county for the paper's annual "progress edition," but the other two were of more than passing interest.

One was a political piece, written by Curt Escobar, exploring the finances of Reese Stevens, an independent candidate for San Bernardino mayor in the last election. Escobar discovered that Stevens—an ardent right-winger who advocated abolishing all social services and reinstating chain gangs to rebuild the county's infrastructure—had relied heavily on contributions from neo-fascist political action committees and paramilitary survivalists to sustain his campaign. The pool of fringe-group money was large enough to give Stevens a war chest more than twice the size of his nearest rival. Someone ought to fumigate this town, Nash thought as he scanned the story.

Among Stevens' few major local supporters was Warren

Construction, which contributed ten thousand dollars to his campaign. The article noted that owner Spice Warren, head of the local John Birch Society chapter, was known for actively supporting conservative political causes.

Nash grabbed the Stevens file next, out of morbid curiosity. He had taken only twelve percent of the popular vote in the general election, despite airing a record number of television ads smearing the other candidates and touting his battle cry: "We Have Just Begun to Fight."

That's what Custer said, Nash thought as he turned back to the last story mentioning Warren Construction. It detailed the mid-day slaying of thirty-five-year-old Shane Littlefeather in front of a used car lot about a year back. Three shots from a .30-06 had torn the man in half while he was using a pay phone. At the time of the article, the police had no suspects or possible motives for the killing. Shane Littlefeather had been Warren's field supervisor. Curiouser and curiouser, Nash thought.

After he put back the construction file, Nash ran a quick check on veterans' counseling centers and Malcolm Snipes, but he found no mention of the deranged drive-in manager in either the old clip drawers or the computer database.

Nash opened his notebook and began jotting down all the follow-up interviews he would have to do: Curt Escobar, Spice Warren, the San Bernardino police. He also wanted to track down the "Mr. Harvey" from Carr's memo about the Hudson's Bay traps. Could Harvey be a representative of the company? Maybe he was from one of the New York auction houses. Maybe he was Carr's invisible rabbit companion.

Finally, Nash wrote down Shane Littlefeather's name followed by a question mark. He didn't want to bother the man's family unless the killing tied in with the Carr story somehow.

And what the hell was the Carr story, anyway? The guy was obviously a rich asshole, but since when had that been a crime in America? Nash was sure there was something weird going on between Snipes and Carr that Carr wasn't talking about. The crazy vet story was strictly made-for-cable. And then there was the business with the trap at the drive-in and Carr's relationship with Spice Warren. And what had Snipes been carrying in those heavy trash bags anyway?

None of it made any sense. What it amounted to was a collection of strange, vindictive people who all had some interest in Carr's drive-in theaters. But why drive-ins? It was time to talk to Escobar.

"Curt, I need your insight," he said. Escobar was sitting in his cubicle, feet propped up on the desk, clicking a pen against his teeth and staring out the window at a meter maid writing a ticket.

"What do you think of this lead?" Escobar asked without turning to face him. "Prior to winning a seat on the City Council under an assumed name, Gregory Baines spent three years in a Mexican jail on heroin charges."

"Shit. When did that happen?"

"It didn't," Escobar said as he swiveled around. "But if that bastard doesn't start returning my calls, I might slip it into the first edition."

"I don't think you'll get that past the copy slot—not to mention the lawyers," Nash said.

Curt grinned and hooked a thumb at his computer screen, which was still blank. "All in good fun," he said. "But I've got a deadline in half an hour and Councilman Baines is probably either on the ninth hole or his fourth martini about now."

"Then you've got a minute?"

"Unless the phone rings. Shoot."

"It's about a story you did last year on Reese Stevens."

"Another classic prick. He raises three million bucks for a mayoral race, spends a million five, tops, then has the stones to hold a post-election fundraiser to 'retire excess campaign debt.' A true American success story."

"Didn't anybody nail him on that?"

"I did," Escobar said. "But then the feds fumbled the investigation. There were never any charges. There never are. What the hell are you messing around with Stevens for anyway?"

"It's this CarrCorp. story."

"You mean the one about the guy in the bear trap at the drive-in?"

"How could I let that go? Right now I'm doing a puff piece on the renovation of Carr's theaters for Faye Krashenko."

"Which lets you stir up the shit a little without raising eyebrows."

"Exactly. But when I went back to the Star-Time to look around yesterday, the manager almost killed me. Then Carr gives me some bullshit story this morning about how this Malcolm Snipes guy is a whacked Vietnam vet Carr takes care of because he's friends with the guy's father."

"If I were you I'd try to make friends with Snipes, too," Escobar said, tapping his pen on Nash's cast.

"Yeah. So then I do a little digging and I find out Spice Warren was the contractor on all three jobs. And since Warren was a big contributor to Reese Stevens' campaign, I thought you might be able to shed a little light."

"It makes sense and it doesn't make sense." Escobar pulled at the edge of his mustache. "It fits in a way because Carr and Warren share the same political leanings. But even if they see eye to eye, I don't see why Warren would be handling these projects. First of all, Carr usually works with another outfit here in town instead of way the hell out to Rancho Cucamonga. And second, as far as I've heard, Warren specializes in office buildings and shopping malls. I've never known him to take on a piss-ant renovation job. Of course, the economy isn't exactly booming here right now."

"But it's worth a closer look?"

"Definitely."

"My next question is, what the hell am I looking for?"

"Ah ha. The crisis of the soul that has afflicted every investigative reporter who ever worked a hunch." Escobar let go of his mustache and went back to tapping his teeth. "When nothing makes sense, you've got to take a step back and look for a bigger picture. If I had to bet, I'd guess that a player like Carr would only seek out someone like Warren if he needed a big job done."

"But he's already got a major contractor in town," Nash said as he wheeled a chair over to Escobar's cubicle.

"Maybe he wants to keep it quiet. So he goes to a smaller company, out of the media spotlight, twenty miles outside of town, owned by a man who shares his rabid political philosophies." Escobar snapped his fingers like he had the wisdom of the ages at his disposal. "Maybe Carr saw some relatively cheap property he could build office buildings or luxury apartments on and he had Warren do all the infrastructure work on the sly."

"Could he do that?"

"Aside from cops busting hookers and dealers, there's not much official presence in the neighborhood around the Star-Time," Escobar said. "And those big fences that keep you from getting a free look at the movie could just as easily hide a lot of heavy construction equipment. When you're done, you just spread on a fresh layer of gravel and build a new snack bar on top."

"Why would he have to do it in secret?"

"Maybe there are zoning problems he plans to get around at some point in the future."

"Okay, but what difference do Warren's politics make?"

"Look, this is all a house of cards," Escobar said between taps. "For all we know, Carr is completely legit on this job and he brought Warren in because he owed him a favor, or his regular outfit was wrapped up on another project. But at least now you've got a working hypothesis to help tie all these coincidences together. So go find some facts to flesh it out."

"Thanks, Curt."

"Don't mention it. By the way, I'd let this thing percolate for a day or so and work on a story for Lydia in the meantime. She's still pissed that you went over to Faye yesterday for that assignment. But if you play cub reporter today, you'll probably get right back on her good side."

Before Nash could get up to leave, Escobar clicked his pen once again and grabbed his cast. "Hold on a sec. I just came up with your nickname." He began scribbling on the plaster. It was one word, written in large, block letters, with cartoon speed lines drawn behind the first letter.

"Rambler?" Nash asked.

"Don't you get it?" Escobar said. "Nash Rambler?"

He held the cast again and drew a set of mag wheels underneath the word. Nash still didn't understand.

"It's a car, man," Escobar said. "Shit. How young are you anyway?"

"Young enough to make you feel old, apparently," Nash rolled his sleeve back down. "Catch you later, pops."

"I'm thirty-two," Escobar said. "And I still eat punks like you for breakfast."

"I bet they go real well with the prunes."

Escobar threw the pen at him.

Nash decided to take Escobar's advice, no matter how meaningless Lydia's latest assignment might be. He found her at the news desk looking over Associated Press photo files for the front page.

"Glad to see you, Nash," she said, putting an arm over his shoulder like a doting professor. "Look here, you might learn something. Did you know that the wire services were pioneers of the facsimile process? It's all online now, but they used to send their shots out as 'laser photos.' I bet you never learned that in your journalism classes."

Actually, Slant had mentioned it in History of Mass Communications, but Nash just nodded as Lydia shared her bits of newspaper trivia.

"Next week, I'll show you some lead letters from the hot-type machine they used here in the fifties," she said. "I want this internship to be a real education for you. It didn't used to be all satellite uplinks and cold type, you know."

"That's great, Lydia. By the way, I was wondering if you might have an extra assignment lying around."

For a moment, he thought she might pinch his cheek. "That's the spirit," she said as she led him to her cubicle. "There's always an assignment waiting for you at the city desk. So don't let any of the other section editors steal you away."

"I'll try not to," he said.

Lydia handed him a press release from the state highway department. As he walked back to his desk she called after him, "Remember, hard news is the life blood of any respectable newspaper."

There was a message waiting for him in his e-mail box.

"Remember, ass kissing is the sustenance of every city editor."

He looked across the room to find Escobar giving him a quick thumbs-up. Nash flipped him off.

The story was about a highway department program to eliminate sexism from road construction signs over a three-year period. At a cost of three hundred thousand, all "Men Working" signs would be changed to "People Working," and "Flagman Ahead" would become "Flagperson Ahead."

One small step for people working, one giant leap for flagpersonkind. Nash began writing out a question sheet for the highway department flack. He wondered how many worthless assignments Lydia would feed him before giving him some real news to cover. His wrist and head began to throb at the same time.

He downed three Tylenol before making the call. "May I speak to media relations, please?" he asked the operator.

"Do you wish to speak to our Image Enhancement Officer?" she replied.

"That would be fine."

It was going to be a long afternoon.

Chapter Eleven

Nash couldn't believe the scene that greeted him when he entered the hallway to his apartment that evening: Three Berdoo Angels from last night's party were re-installing the front door. At least he thought they were Angels; their paint-flecked work clothes made it hard to picture them in full biker denims.

The Angel Nash had last seen cutting his face with a butterfly knife was spackling a small hole in the living-room wall. The man who had been holding the skull bong was replacing the glass door to the balcony with minimal assistance from his strung-out girlfriend. And a guy he didn't recognize was running a Rug Doctor over the beer-soaked carpet.

He tried to imagine a more surreal scene. Perhaps he would find Mr. Clean and the Scrubbing Bubbles scouring his bathroom.

"Aren't these guys great?" Homer hollered from down the hall. He was carefully scrubbing the spray-painted skull and crossbones off Nash's bedroom door.

"I'm speechless," Nash replied, evading the Rug Doctor as he made his way down the hall. "They even look like human beings."

"They're mostly just regular guys like me." Homer said this without irony as he slopped the scrub brush in a bucket of brown suds. "They've got families and kids and straight jobs. Sure, they let it all hang out after work and on the weekends, but it's basically just a stress-relief thing."

"A little marauding is good for the soul," Nash said, turning back to look at the perverse band of helper elves in the living room. Skull Bong waved at him, and Butterfly Knife gave him a two-fingered salute before going back to the spackle. "Did those cops arrest you?"

"No. They just broke the party up. It's a pretty regular occurrence around here. The landlady's not mad, either. She was at her sister's last night and it looks like nobody complained except for whoever called the cops."

"Great. So I can expect carnage like this every week until somebody files felony charges?"

"I promise I won't abuse our friendship like that again," Homer said in a somber tone.

"Wait, I'll get my tape recorder."

Homer crossed his heart with the scrub brush, feigning an earnest look as a mass of suds dripped down his shirt.

"All right, all right," Nash said. "Just don't mess with me like this again."

"Agreed," Homer said cheerily. He gave Nash a sudsy handshake and went back to scrubbing the door.

To get away from the Night of the Living Housekeepers, Nash decided to explore one of Carr's other theaters and get some color for the feature he had to write for Faye Krashenko. Wendy was working an evening shift, so he went to the drive-in alone for the first time in his life.

Walking among the beer-swilling, heavy-petting teenagers and the young families sitting on lawn chairs in the backs of trucks, Nash felt like a social outcast. He had reported a great many events as a freelancer and he'd usually had a good time doing it. But there was always a barrier between him and the rest of the crowd. As a journalist, he was forced to experience everything at a distance. And although reporting allowed him to feel comfortably aloof, it often left him emotionally off-balance and out of sync with the rest of humanity as well.

Tonight, the thought of being more than two thousand miles from home made his loneliness even more acute. He wanted to call some of his friends, maybe even Slant, who understood better than most the reporter's odd feelings of detachment. But it was two hours later in Chicago, too late for a philosophical discussion that probably wouldn't do him much good anyway.

Nash tried to evade his loneliness by throwing himself into the job at hand. He walked around the snack bar and the theater grounds recording details and impressions for another half-hour before climbing back into the 2002. Without thinking, he turned on the headlights as he started the engine. With dozens of car horns blaring at him, Nash killed the lights and headed for the exit, behind the concession stand.

He ground to a halt next to the building and thought about how Snipes had crushed his wrist behind the Star-Time snack bar. But that wasn't the memory that was bothering him.

Then he had it. The family. The dead family was found in the trash behind a supermarket near the drive-in the night Ronald Slasnik got his foot caught in the bear trap. And Snipes had left Nash behind the Dumpster at the neighborhood Von's.

Son-of-a-bitch. The words formed slowly in his head. The story was moving rapidly past zoning violations and simple assault. First, Spice Warren's field supervisor, Shane Littlefeather, had been shot. And then three people had turned up dead—likely in the exact spot where Malcolm Snipes later tossed Nash. But even if the killings were connected somehow, that was an awfully high body count for a construction cover-up.

Suddenly, the numb feeling came back. Nash had an overpowering urge to drive until he lost himself in the hazy neon of the L.A. skyline.

Afraid he would get trapped in the confusing grid of freeways, Nash turned toward the mountains instead, heading northwest on a quiet two-lane and thinking through the investigation's next move. Twenty minutes later he reached the hillside community of Lytle Creek. He stopped by the town's roadside tavern, a homey relic with a wood stove for cool winter nights and a barmaid who offered him a steaming plate of homemade chicken and dumplings. They were the best he'd tasted, and the beer was cool and smooth.

Nash played a game of pool with two sleepy-eyed locals who grooved to Eagles tunes on the jukebox between shots. Then he grabbed another beer and headed for the front porch. An old man in a checked shirt and suspenders sat in a rocking chair singing a gentle nonsense song to himself over and over, pausing now and then to bring a glass of beer to his lips with quivering hands. The barmaid called him Dusty. It was somehow reassuring, listening to Dusty murmur and rock as he worked on the beer.

After a few minutes, Dusty noticed Nash staring at him, and for a moment he came back from wherever he'd been. He stared back at Nash intently.

"Seems like a young one like you would have something better to do than sit on this porch feeling sorry for yourself with nothing but ghosts and drunks for company," Dusty said. His few strands of brittle black hair refused to lie flat on his head, but he had a big, toothy smile. "If I had your legs, I'd be chasing down every young girl I saw and getting into every sort of trouble. I'd be running just to feel the wind."

As Nash drove back down the hill, he felt a renewed sense of purpose. Dusty was right. He was here to gain experience as a reporter and to make a name for himself—and he wouldn't mind improving the world as much as he could along the way.

He knew that if he kept pressing the investigation, he was bound to come up with a more important story than he'd ever find in a playground or highway department press release. Maybe he'd even help four spirits rest a little easier.

By the time he got back to the apartment, the mop-up was complete and there was a message on his answering machine from Wendy.

"The bed's too big without you," was all she said, but that was more than enough.

Go get 'em tiger, Nash thought as he padded down the hall to Wendy's apartment with his pillow tucked under his arm.

Later, they were both too keyed-up to sleep, so Wendy shared the events of her evening at Denny's while Nash rubbed her feet. An off-duty cop having a cup of coffee had nabbed a group of kids when they tried to skip out on their check. The cute new assistant manager had asked out one of the waitresses, a friend of hers. Another cook had quit. And some guy had grabbed a huge handful of candy from the March of Dimes charity bin and then dropped a penny into the coin slot.

"It made me so sad when he did that, I almost cried," Wendy said, arching her back slightly when Nash hit a pressure point near her big toe.

"Did you yell at him?"

"They fire us if we talk back to the customers."

"Not much you can do in a situation like that." Nash crawled up her body and kissed her nose.

"But I did do something," she said. "I put some of my tip money in the box later. Those sick babies need every cent they can get."

Nash pulled the covers up over their shoulders and snuggled in close. "You're too cool for that place," he said. "They should at least give you time off for good behavior."

"I'm off tomorrow."

"Then you are a very lucky woman."

"How's that?"

"I'm going to go see the Cubs play the Dodgers tomorrow night, and I just happen to have an extra ticket."

"Great. I've been a Dodgers fan ever since they beat Oakland in the '88 World Series." Wendy sat up in bed, remembering. "My dad took me to one of the games. Kirk Gibson was my favorite."

"That's okay sweetheart, I won't hold it against you."

"You're not a Cubs fan, are you?" Wendy asked. "What a bunch of losers."

"Hey, I'm from Chicago. What do you expect?" He turned to look up at her. "The only thing we North Siders all share besides our love for the Cubs is a hatred for teams from California."

"Then we might as well make this interesting." She was grinning.

"What did you have in mind?"

"Friendly wager. If the Dodgers win, you stay out here with me an extra week after your internship ends."

"And what if the Cubbies take it?"

"I'll come back to Chicago with you for a while."

"Better start packing your bags."

"So you accept?"

"I do," Nash said solemnly. With his good hand, he began tickling her side until, squirming with laughter, she managed to stop him with her kisses.

"Would you like to try for a double-header?" Wendy asked as she rolled on top of him.

"Am I still the designated hitter?"

"Why don't you put on another batting glove and find out."

Chapter Twelve

Nash awoke to pounding on the door of Wendy's apartment. As she stirred beside him, he pushed off the arm she'd flopped across his chest in her sleep.

"You in there, Nash?" Homer yelled from the other side of the door, two rooms away. "Your boss is on the phone and she sounds pissed."

Brought to full alert by Homer's voice, Nash pulled on a pair of running shorts and bolted for the living room. He opened the front door before his roommate could start to beat on it again.

"My boss always sounds pissed," Nash said. "It's seven A.M. and it's Wendy's day off. Can't you just tell Lydia I'll be in by nine?"

Homer shook his head. "No way, man. She scares me."

After kissing his half-asleep girlfriend on the forehead, Nash followed Homer back to their apartment. When he picked up the phone, he heard instrumental hold music—it sounded like a Muzak version of Britney Spears' "Oops . . . I Did It Again"—so he hung up.

Not thirty seconds later, as Nash was grabbing a box of cereal from the cupboard, the phone rang.

"First you're not available when I call and then you hang up on me?" Lydia Sorenson said when he picked up the phone.

Nash decided submissive was always the right play with

her. "Sorry," he said. "All I heard was music."

"When you have a paper to run, sometimes you have to put people on hold," she lectured. "Just try to be there the next time I call."

"Will do." Nash gouged out Cap'n Crunch's face with his free thumb. "Do you need me to come in early?"

"I need you out in the field ASAP. A kid just got suspended from a local high school over a violent art project. TV's already on it, but I think it'll make a great A-1 lead for tomorrow."

Finally, Nash thought, a real assignment. "That sounds great, Lydia. Thanks."

"Don't mention it. You were sixteen yourself not too long ago, so I figure you stand the best chance of establishing a strong rapport with the kid. I talked to his mom. They're expecting you in half an hour."

"When do I need to have the story finished?" he asked.

"Oh, right," Lydia said. "I haven't laid it all out for you yet: I'm going to have one of my real reporters write the story. You can just turn your notes in to me when you get here."

Nash punched the cereal box across the room.

"What was that?" Lydia asked.

"Nothing, Lydia. Just grabbing my notebook."

After she gave him the teen's name and address, Nash set the receiver gently back in place. He wasn't going to let Lydia tear him down with her sadistic mind games. This was still a meaty story. And if he toed the line, he might even get a "with reporting by" credit at the end of it.

He knew he'd make the front page soon enough. Hard work had to win the day at some point. He tried smiling at himself in the bathroom mirror, but all he could muster was a grimace.

★ ★ ★ ★ ★

Nash arrived at the suspended student's home just as a live-remote TV truck was pulling out. They might get it faster, he thought, but we'll get the full story.

Before he could knock, a woman, probably the boy's mother, opened the door and waved him in. As he stepped onto the green shag rug of the living room, the woman placed her hand over the cordless receiver she was holding. "I'm on with morning radio in L.A.," she said. "Brad's in his room, on the computer like always." She pointed down a short hallway, toward the doorway on the right. "Why don't you go in and talk with him, and we'll catch up in a bit."

Sure enough, Brad was hunkered down in front of an old desktop PC in a room messier than any college dorm Nash had ever seen. The computer case was covered with stickers from punk bands ranging from old-schoolers The Germs to more recent acts like Rage Against the Machine and Anti-Flag.

Straddling a backwards-facing metal folding chair, the teen looked up long enough to nod Nash in and say, "Close the door behind you." With his braided hair and skate-punk garb, Brad looked like he'd jumped straight from the pages of *Thrasher* magazine, but a gleam of mischievous intellect in his eyes belied his slacker appearance.

"You with the paper?" he asked as Nash moved in for a look at the screen.

"Yeah," he replied. Brad was playing *The Sims*, a computer game that gave users godlike control over every aspect of the characters' lives.

"I heard you got suspended for pissing off your art instructor," Nash said loudly enough to be heard over the Dead Kennedys MP3 blaring from the PC's speakers.

"More like I freaked her out," Brad said as he turned the

sound down a notch. "I didn't mean to, but I lucked into a two-week vacation."

Nash watched, entranced, as Sim hours sped by in seconds. The colorful little men, women, children, and infants demanded Brad's help in meeting their most picayune needs. But he didn't seem to care much for them.

As Nash looked on, houses were burgled, carpools were missed, kitchens were lit afire, and all the while Sim bladders filled to bursting, dinner remnants were left to rot on the floor near overflowing garbage cans, and newspapers sat outside unread and yellowing. Even while doing so little for themselves, the constantly complaining people would grow so tired they would drop where they stood until they gained enough energy to wake up and rail once more at their unseen, incompetent protector.

Brad told Nash how he made life even more miserable for these pixilated people who mewled in gibberish as lightning bolts flashed in thought bubbles above their heads. One family he imprisoned in a house with no windows or doors—only a refrigerator that never ran out of food. Another lived on a fully furnished lot, but with no house to hide their beds, couches, sinks, and toilets.

The wrathful teen had even figured out several creative ways to kill his Sims. Installing a swimming pool only to remove the ladders after the bathers dove in was a surefire way to destroy them. The animated creatures would swim for hours of Sim time, building up strength and fitness points until their energy reserves ran down to zero and they drowned, exhausted. Brad enlivened this tortuous display by outfitting his swimmers in Speedos and Sherlock Holmes hats, which stayed dry until their noggins went under for the last time.

But Brad had devised more devious extermination methods as well. For instance, he built a brick chimney around one unsuspecting artificial man and then installed a grill. Minutes ticked by in real time as the Sim-man's hunger raged. He was smart enough to know he shouldn't fire up the barbecue, but too famished to resist the promise of succulent simulated steak, and so came to an explosive end.

"I've gotten one electrocuted by having him repair a broken TV, but that takes forever and it's usually an actual accident," Brad said.

There was a knock at the door. Brad waited a beat before finally granting a "Come in." It was his mother.

"Don't let him turn you into a murderer with that game," she said. "If he wasn't so sweet-natured, I'd think he was a serial killer the way he tortures those poor cartoon people. Although it is kind of funny when he drowns the ones with the pipes and detective hats."

"It's Sherlock Holmes, Mom," Brad said. "The hats."

"That's what I meant, honey. But I do need to talk to this gentleman for a minute. Can you spare him?"

"Just shut the door behind you," Brad said, eyes still trained on the screen. "I can't stand how noisy this house is."

"Does he always make you wait like that when you knock?" Nash asked as they made their way back into the living room.

She nodded. "Testing his turf power. But believe me, when it comes to sixteen-year-old boys, you want to give them advance notice before you open the door on them anyway." She stopped. "I haven't introduced myself. I'm Pam Lapham."

"Nash Hansen, from the *Ledger*."

"So they sent us a boy reporter." She smiled. "Smart. I'm sure Brad has you well-initiated into the world of Sims by now."

"Unfortunately, yes, he has. But we hadn't got around to discussing the art project yet."

"Oh, well, you were looking at it," she said. "He brought screen captures of his dying Sims into art class. The teacher was so alarmed by what she saw that she alerted the counselor. To cover his ass, the counselor told the assistant principal, and the assistant principal suspended Brad."

"They booted him out for screen captures?"

"Yes. Pictures of animated people on fire. That's apparently a crime now. He also brought one with two male Sims in bed together. How utterly shocking. But they said violent and inappropriate images are warning signs." Pam Lapham shook her head. "Warning signs that he's a button-pushing teenager without a lick of sense, that's what they are. And that didn't used to get you suspended from school for two weeks."

"Can you appeal?" Nash asked.

"We're meeting with the principal tomorrow. After that, we'll take it up with the school board, I guess."

Chapter Thirteen

When Nash sat down at his Sims-free computer at ten A.M., he found an ominous e-mail from Curt Escobar waiting for him: "Watch out, Rambler, you're about to get Tattooed." He looked around the office, but the political reporter was nowhere to be found. Just as Nash was about to start trying to find a source at the police department, Lydia came storming toward him from the direction of the publisher's office.

"Mr. Hansen," she said as she came into earshot, "we need to talk about a suspension." She was waving a pink memo sheet at him like she was trying to shake something sticky off her hands.

"I've got the quotes for you right here," he said, waving back at her with his notebook.

"I've just spoken to the publisher about you," she said as she advanced on him and grabbed the notes.

Remembering the last time Lydia had cornered him at his desk, Nash stood up so she couldn't block him in. "What's wrong?" he asked, taking on what he hoped was the reasonable tone of a man who knows there has been a terrible misunderstanding, one that he plans to clear up immediately.

"How dare you play stupid with me," she hissed. Lydia's stubby fingernails were digging into the palms of her hands. The pressure was turning the tips of her fingers white.

"Okay, start at the beginning," he said, taking a step back.

"Evan Carr called me this morning to complain about how you harassed him and his employees."

"I don't believe this."

"Believe it. It's going to be a rough ride." She thrust the memo at him. "I've written up a report of your transgressions and, in conference with the publisher, Mr. Clancy, I am removing you from active reporting duty, effective immediately. You are about a millimeter away from getting your ass busted all the way back to Chicago."

The words hit Nash with the force of a Malcolm Snipes kick to the abdomen. He felt queasy and lightheaded. He needed to sit down.

"This is wrong," he said. In five minutes, Carr had completely destroyed his reputation.

"You're damn right it's wrong," Lydia said as Nash eased himself into his chair. "I wanted to fire you on the spot and report you to your advisers at Northwestern, but Mr. Clancy wants to give you another chance. He called Evan Carr, and the man was gracious enough to ask that you be kept on in a non-reporting capacity."

"Is that final?" He couldn't believe this was coming down so quickly.

"Well, let's see, Nash. You trespassed at the Star-Time and then assaulted the manager when he asked you to leave. You spied on Mr. Carr's private papers during an interview and then you insulted him. Is that final enough for you?"

He could see no point in resisting now. It was his word against Carr's, and there were enough half-truths in everything he had said to make an adequate defense impossible. Carl Barns had offered to help, but Nash could see no benefit in asking the photographer to detail the unpleasant exchange he'd overheard.

"It looks like your mind's made up," he said.

81

"You were interviewing him for a fucking feature, Nash. What reason would he have to attack you? Give me a motive that I can believe and I'll check it out. But if you're wasting my time, you'll be lucky to find a job selling ads for the *Penny Saver* after I'm through with you."

Nash knew a list of his suspicions and hunches would make Lydia go completely ballistic. At the very least, she would tip Carr off and ruin the investigation. At worst, she might try to get him kicked out of school. Because this was his for-credit internship, he was already looking at paying for an extra quarter if she gave him a failing assessment. And he was carrying more loan debt than most Third World countries as it was.

"What if I write Carr a personal apology and give Faye Krashenko a glowing report on his drive-ins?" Admittedly, it was a last-ditch effort, but any compromise that kept him writing longer would be to his benefit.

"I expect you to apologize, but that's not going to change the situation." She paused to think over his second offer. "All right. Finish the feature. Maybe one positive thing will come out of this mess. But that's it on the reporting. After you turn in the piece, you'll serve a week's suspension and then report to the copy desk for the rest of your internship."

"If that's the way it has to be."

"You'd better make the most of the experience," Lydia said as she started to back away. "Or I'll beat you like a tin drum."

After she left, Nash realized that everyone in the newsroom had been watching the scene. Screw them all, he thought as he gave the remaining onlookers a wave. Carr wouldn't be putting on this kind of heat unless he was onto something bad and ugly. This one had teeth. And bad breath.

Nash had bought himself a few extra days of legitimate reporting to finish the bulk of the investigation: It was now Wednesday morning and the story was due on Monday. After that, he would turn into a pumpkin as far as his editors were concerned.

Speaking of editors, he knew he'd better update Faye Krashenko about the shambles he'd managed to make of the drive-in piece. Better to take all his lumps at one time, he thought as he made his way to the features department.

Faye looked up from a color page proof as he was about to apologize and share his troubles.

"Don't bother," she said as he opened his mouth. "I already know the sordid details—including the lack of support from the powers that be here at the *Ledger*. And yes, I still want you to write the story. Curt Escobar told me you're good people, and he's one of the shrewdest—as well as nicest—guys in the newsroom."

"This means a lot," Nash said. "Thanks."

"I wish it meant more," Faye said. "I was brought up in this business to watch my colleagues' backs. If you really did what Evan Carr claims, well, a suspension is justified. But if it's the old gambit of a powerful person doing everything he can to keep the local press under his thumb—and that's what it smells like—then Lydia's reaction is shameful. From the sounds of it, she convicted you as soon as he called."

"At least I'll have one good clip to take back to school with me."

"Lydia's managed to piss off a lot of colleagues with her abrasive manner," Faye said. "If you write a strong, balanced feature, that might give me enough ammunition to speak to the publisher on your behalf. At the very least, maybe he'll let me assign you a few more stories for my section."

"I'd owe you more than that," Nash said.

Faye started to wave him off, but then smiled to herself.

"There is one thing you can do for me," she said.

"Name it."

"Curt seems to have taken you under his wing."

"That's true."

The features editor blushed, but pressed on. "Since you've got his ear," she said, "please tell him to stop being such a stranger."

On the walk back to city-side, Nash didn't sense that everyone in the newsroom was against him like he had before his talk with Faye. Maybe he could turn this thing around after all.

"Bad news, Rambler," Escobar said when Nash reached his cubicle. "Would you like a Twinkie? They always make me feel better."

Nash opened the bag Escobar had pulled out of his sport-coat pocket, then handed one of the cakes back to him. "Thanks, Curt," he said between bites. "Faye tells me you're still on my side."

"Now more than ever, *compadre*." Escobar polished his Twinkie off with the second bite. Pausing to swallow, he continued to gesture as he chewed, too excited to quit talking. "You've really hit a nerve here. I'd like to help continue the surgery. Running your first real investigation will be the best type of learning experience you could get here. But I'll be ready to step in if the going gets too rough."

Nash told him about his source list and the time constraint. Escobar took careful notes throughout the conversation and rattled off more possible avenues for investigation than Nash could keep track of.

"So what can I do here?" Escobar asked.

"Get me in contact with someone on the police force who can tell me more about the trap incident, Evan Carr,

Malcolm Snipes, the Shane Littlefeather killing, the family in the Dumpster, and anything else I might think of."

"Done." Curt re-opened his notebook. "Any leads you want me to follow up?"

"I want to know more about the relationship between Evan Carr and Spice Warren and the right-wing groups who supported that scumbag mayoral candidate, what's his name?"

"Reese Stevens."

"Right. I think Malcolm Snipes might be tied in with one of those paramilitary groups," Nash continued. "I know I'm not the toughest guy in the world, but Snipes handled me like a pro. And he was spouting something about his Constitutional rights while he was doing it."

"I'll see what I can dig up." Escobar placed a hand on Nash's shoulder. "By the way, I checked the phone books of every community within fifty miles and I didn't find one Snipes."

Nash felt his cheeks redden. "I didn't even think of that," he said.

"Watch and learn. Anyway, if I had to guess, I'd say Snipes, if that's even his real name, doesn't have a dad who pals around with Carr."

"Another chink in the armor."

Escobar nodded. "Just remember, this is likely to get a whole lot worse before it gets better."

"Why are you putting yourself on the line like this, Curt?"

"I'm getting sick of council meetings and bond issues. Besides, I really think Lydia's full of shit on this one, and I'd like to see her get knocked down a peg or two. Why don't we take a late lunch and call on a friend of mine on the force?"

Chapter Fourteen

The officer in charge of the police department's sprawling file room, a man in his thirties with bluish teeth and a rickety gait, looked like he had already pulled one too many night shifts. He had the pale hue that comes from years spent under fluorescent lights, and, although his arms were excessively thin, a small pot belly hung over the top of his belt.

"Hello, Curt," he said slowly as they walked into the room. "What can I do you for?" He was sucking a can of orange juice through a miniature straw. A half-eaten pastrami sandwich rested on the edge of a dusty file cabinet.

"Afternoon, Klete," Escobar said. He gave the officer a slap on the back and gestured toward Nash. "I'd like you to meet an associate of mine, Nash Hansen. Nash, this is Officer Klete Patterson." As Nash shook the officer's hand, Escobar pulled a strand of pastrami out of the sandwich and popped it into his mouth.

"I want you to extend all the same courtesies to old Nash here as you do to me," he said as he chewed. "He's a little wet yet, so you might have to show him around the files."

The officer nodded several times as Escobar spoke. Twice Patterson cast an apprehensive glance Nash's way, reminding him of a nervous dog, eager to please, expecting to be punished.

"You gonna eat the rest of this sandwich?" Escobar asked. He picked it up off the cabinet and took a huge bite.

"I guess not," Patterson said, scratching his left arm through the sleeve of his uniform.

"You got something to wash this down, maybe?" Escobar pointed the sandwich at a mini-refrigerator humming loudly next to Patterson's desk.

The officer got out another orange juice. Before handing it to Escobar, he peeled off the aluminum tab and carefully dropped a straw into the can. By the time Patterson had completed these simple tasks, Escobar was finished with the sandwich.

"Thanks," he grunted as he licked a slick of mayonnaise off his upper lip. "Hey, you been working out?"

"No. Why?"

"You're lookin' mean and lean is all."

"And clean," the officer said, smiling for the first time since they'd walked in.

"Good, good," Escobar replied. "Now, would you be so kind as to pull any files past or present concerning the people on this list?"

"You want those now?" Patterson asked as he took the sheet of paper from Escobar. "I'm on my lunch."

"Doesn't look like there's much lunch around here to eat," Escobar said, winking at Nash. "Why don't you have photocopies of the whole shooting match ready for us by three, okay?"

"Sure, Curt. They'll be here when you get back." With that, the officer began poring over the list and punching information into the computer with his right index finger.

"Pretty good service, don't you think?" Escobar asked as they left the station. He finished off the orange juice and made a clean jumper into a trash can about twenty feet down the sidewalk.

"What the hell do you have on that guy?" Nash had heard of pet sources, but this was extreme.

"Hasn't anyone ever told you that information is power?" Escobar replied as they climbed into his convertible Skylark.

"Must be some serious shit."

"I've owned Klete's ass ever since he started working in the evidence room several years ago." Escobar checked his teeth in the rearview mirror as they turned onto the expressway. "I started out here as a night cops reporter, and my first big splash was a series on theft from the police evidence cage. I ended up nailing eight cops."

"Including Klete?"

"No. Klete was the ninth cop I sniffed out, but I made sure he was never implicated in the official investigation. The rest all did hard time."

"Why'd you let him off the hook?"

"The other guys were taking huge amounts of drugs out of evidence and peddling them on the street. A few were also fencing stolen goods and pocketing as much loose cash as they could get their hands on. But Klete was different." Escobar paused to work a bit of pastrami out of his teeth with his pinkie. "He was your basic honest rookie, until his partner turned him onto amphetamines to help him through the graveyard shift. He developed a rather nasty habit, which he naturally fed by dipping into the endless supply of crystal meth that passed through the cage every day. Basically, the guy couldn't help himself."

"But he was still a dirty cop."

"Let's just say he was a lighter shade of gray than the others. He only took junk for personal use. He never sold it and he never took any property out of the room. Plus, the guy never missed a fucking shift. He processed more shit in and out of that cage than any three cops could have. He was a real credit to the force."

"Is he still using?" Nash asked. "He looks like hell."

"Nah, he's just a lazy son of a bitch."

"How do you know he quit?"

"By the time I confronted old Klete, his teeth were already rotting out of his head—speed'll do that to you—and he was developing a hell of a nervous twitch. The guy wanted out pretty bad. So I made a deal with him: He helped me out with the investigation, anonymously of course, and I not only let him off the hook, I paid for six weeks of out-patient rehab."

"From your own pocket?"

"Are you kidding?" Escobar shook his head. "I put the whole thing on my expense account. Then, after the series won three awards for reporting excellence, the accountants finally got around to questioning the expenditure. I hinted to the editor that I had a great offer from the *Orange County Register* and gave him the impression that I'd just as soon go as stay. My expenses were approved the next day and they promoted me to the political beat. Award-winning series are better than sex for most editors. Deliver them on a regular basis, and you'll write your own ticket."

"Quite a racket," Nash said.

"They don't give out awards for ethics in this business. Well, they do, but who gives a crap about them?"

"Why'd you have to step on Klete so hard?" Nash asked.

"He's been making a lot of noise lately about debts fulfilled and all that jazz," Escobar replied. "So I had to remind him that I hold a long-term lease on his soul. I have tape, I have photos, and he knows it. Remember, I kept him out of prison, and I helped him get clean. Deep down, he's still grateful to me. I just have to keep bringing that gratitude to the surface."

"That's a tough attitude."

"It's tough to get people to actually sit down and read something these days, Rambler. You've got to deliver a blockbuster report if you want them to go past the headline. And that means developing great sources—and keeping them. Remember, print is on its way out."

"People have been saying that ever since Marconi introduced the radio," Nash said. "And yet, today people read tons of stuff on the Web, they buy more books than ever . . ."

"You know why people read on the toilet?" Escobar interrupted.

"I never thought to ask."

"They're multitasking."

"I guess so," Nash said.

"That's the only way they can allow themselves time to read. They figure, 'I'm just sitting here waiting for my bodily functions to finish, so I don't have to feel guilty about wasting time reading.' We've put reading so far down on the scale of acceptable activities that the only time you can crack a book without feeling like you're missing something is when you're on the toilet, the Stairmaster, the bus, or the beach. It's disgusting."

"I'm sure there are some people who love reading so much that they read in the bathroom in addition to lots of other places," Nash said. "At the breakfast table, in bed, on the bus . . ."

"But those are all examples of multitasking," Escobar replied.

"Except the bed."

"That just proves our culture values getting a good night's sleep even less than reading."

"I guess you're right."

"I mean, when's the last time you or anyone you knew just stayed in for an evening or a Saturday afternoon to read a book for pleasure?" Escobar asked. "Turned off the TV, let the lawn grow for another day, and just read?"

"Well, there are those book groups Oprah made so popular. People devote an evening a week to those."

"Sure, they'll spend quality time discussing books with other people—it's a social event—but I'll bet you money they only actually read the books while they're doing something more important."

"Like taking a crap," Nash said, laughing.

"You don't think that's important?" Escobar asked. "Wait a few years."

When Nash began sorting through the short stack of police files in his apartment late that afternoon, he couldn't help feeling guilty about having been party to such abuse. Still, he thought, there might be enough leverage in the reports to find out why Evan Carr and Malcolm Snipes were so upset at drawing a reporter's attention.

Nash was jolted out of his sleep by a knock on the door. He sat up, disoriented. It took him a moment to realize he was on the couch amidst the police reports. He checked his watch. Six o'clock. He hadn't been out long. The knock came again.

He opened the door to find Wendy in blue shorts and a blue cotton tank top. Even with the Dodgers cap on her head, he had to admit she looked cute.

"C'mon," she said. "I don't want to miss the game."

Chapter Fifteen

Even though he disliked the pompous Dodgers on principle, Nash had to admire the sense of tradition permeating Dodger Stadium. As he and Wendy parked in a remote lot, he noticed the vaunted Dodger Blue on display everywhere. And when they found their seats on the second level of the four-tiered park, he noticed the large white letters spelling out "Think Blue" on the palm-lined hill behind the left-field wall.

"They've still got the cotton candy," Wendy said, pointing out a vendor carrying a tray of sky blue spun sugar.

Nash had picked up a more traditional combo of a foot-long Dodger Dog and a beer. Even without a brick backstop or ivy on the outfield wall, these classic elements of the game were still honored at Chavez Ravine.

"At least the Cubs will be up first." He balanced the hot dog on his left knee and put his right arm around Wendy's shoulder.

She reached up to squeeze his hand and said, "Here in California we always save the best for last."

A rookie shortstop led off for the Cubs. A giant picture of his face and hitting stats came up on the Diamond Vision screen as Kevin Brown stepped onto the pitcher's mound.

"I've never seen a Cub three stories high before," Nash said as the rook took a bad swing at a nasty curve to open the game.

"Welcome to the twenty-first century."

"So your dad used to take you out here?"

"Just that one time, for the World Series game in '88. He was a big fan, but he would never make the drive from Sacramento for a regular game."

"How'd he get Series tickets?"

"Dad ran a tire dealership. Goodyear took him and a bunch of other managers to the game. He wasn't supposed to bring any guests, but he figured no one would keep a cute little eight-year-old from enjoying her first trip to the ballpark."

The Cubs had made two outs during the conversation. The number-three hitter stepped up to the plate.

"Sosa's the man." Nash pointed his hot dog toward the right fielder's .300 average and bushel basket of homers displayed on the Diamond Vision.

"He's not as good as Brown, I'd bet," Wendy said.

On the first pitch, she was right. A smoking fastball caught the inside edge of the dish for a called strike.

On the next pitch, Slammin' Sammy lined out to right. Wendy leaned over and planted a playful kiss on Nash. An old man sitting on the other side of her gave him an approving nod before turning back to his scorecard.

"No fair distracting the visiting team," Nash said.

"Don't worry, it won't happen again." Wendy scrunched her nose. "You taste like mustard."

At the seventh-inning stretch, the Cubs led the Dodgers 2-1. Nash flagged down a peanut vendor, who sailed a bag right into his hands from two rows away. The kid's prowess earned him applause from the surrounding fans—as well as a dollar tip from Nash. Even though Sosa had hammered a two-run blast 395 feet to center in his second at-bat, the game had turned into a pitcher's duel between Brown and Kerry Wood. It was definitely peanut-chewing time.

"You're not ready to leave yet, are you?" Nash asked. "Every time I watch a Dodgers game on TV, half the fans are heading for the exits with their beach balls by the middle of the fifth." He pointed to a family doing just that.

"Not me," Wendy said. "I'm waiting for the big rally."

"Just don't try to start the Wave."

"You sure are young to be such a curmudgeon."

"Like the sign says, Think Blue."

"Are you worried about a story?"

He nodded. "I've been investigating a real estate developer in connection with a possible corrupt business deal."

"No wonder you're stressed out. That's a pretty big piece to work on in your first week."

"That's not it, Wendy. I've gone to school for almost six years to learn how to do this stuff. And I've been freelancing stories even longer than that."

"Then what's the problem?"

"The developer told my editor I've been harassing him. So the publisher suspended me from my reporting duties."

"That's terrible. How are you going to handle it?"

"See the story through. Even if I have to do it on my own time. The *Ledger*'s political reporter has been helping with the investigation."

"Is there anything I can do?" Wendy drew him close and kissed his cheek.

"You're doing it right now."

"So this would be even better?" she asked, brushing his lips with hers. She moved in for a kiss that took two pitches to complete.

He wanted it to continue all the way through the batting order, but a troubling thought brought him up for air. "I've never been what you'd call smooth with the ladies," he said. "So why'd you latch onto me so quickly?"

"You ate two meals in a row at Denny's just to see me again. That's truly flattering."

"Seriously, though."

Wendy cocked her head at him. "We've already established that you don't see me as a slut," she said. "And even if you're not Mr. Smooth, you are pretty damn confident in your approach. So if something's bothering you, it's got to be about Bill."

Nash nodded. She was more perceptive than a lot of his classmates.

Wendy continued. "Is she just doing this to get revenge on the man who done her wrong? Is this a classic rebound case? Is this gum-cracking waitress just setting me up for a fall? Am I close?"

Nash laughed. "I haven't seen you crack any gum. But otherwise, yeah, close enough."

"You are some piece of work, Mr. Hansen. Here you are, a cub reporter on a whirlwind tour of Southern California, and you're worried about *my* long-term intentions? That's a good one."

She was right, of course. But when it came to relationships, Nash had always been a glommer. Flings made him uncomfortable. Obviously, though, she was an attractive young woman who'd recently been dumped, and he was here on a three-month adventure. The math was so simple it didn't bear double-checking.

"Why don't we just enjoy ourselves and see how it unfolds?" she said. "While my intentions might be hazy, they certainly are pure. I really like you. I can play tour guide and show you all my favorite spots, you like to talk about writing . . . besides, you're cute as hell."

Nash felt his face redden. "Isn't that supposed to be my line?" he asked.

She shrugged. "New century, new rules."

On the field, Kevin Brown bunted into an inning-ending double play.

"New rules are fine by me," Nash said. "As long as the National League doesn't add the designated hitter."

Somehow, the Cubs still found a way to lose.

"It's lucky you didn't bet any money on the game," Wendy said. She touched a beer bottle to her forehead while handing another one to Nash.

"If you keep gloating like that, I'll wish I did owe you a twenty instead of an extra week out here," he said. Nash took a long pull on his MGD. "*This* is the pause that refreshes."

"Sorry it's so hot in here." She was standing behind him now, rubbing his right shoulder with her free hand. "At least we spent the evening outside. Coming home to this hotbox after a shift at freezing goddamn Denny's is the worst of both worlds."

"Speaking of Denny's," Nash said, "I've always wondered, do you get a lot of guys in there looking for a free meal on their birthday?"

"It's usually just rowdy teens and old people," Wendy said. "Looking forward to a free birthday meal is probably the only thing they have in common."

"And do you tend to remember your customers from one day to the next?"

"I've got a few regulars. Why?"

"I just think it would be a great scam to get three-hundred-sixty-five fake IDs—well, three-hundred-sixty-four, actually—each one with a different birthday . . ."

"So you could eat free at Denny's every day of the year?"

He crooked his head back at her and smiled.

"You are a freak, no doubt about it," she said. But she leaned in to kiss him anyway.

"Would they catch me, do you think?" Nash asked.

"I'd catch you, yeah. But I wouldn't tell."

"So all I have to do is find a waitress who thinks I'm cute?"

She thumped him, lightly, on the shoulder. "Is that all I am to you? Free Grand Slam breakfasts?"

"Yeah, I've got other girls for lunch and dinner." He stood up and moved in to kiss her again.

"Don't you think it's too hot for that?" she asked.

"We can open a window," he said.

Later, Nash sat on the edge of the tub with another cold beer and watched Wendy color her hair. The pale skin of her arms and legs made the royal blue towel she wore look drab by comparison.

It was as nice a domestic scene as he'd been part of since the summer after junior year, when he and his high school girlfriend had tried to rekindle their romance by renting a lake house in Wisconsin. The reunion had its moments, but they'd changed too much to make it stick. That was more than two years ago, and he hadn't had a relationship worth remembering since.

The smell of ammonia brought Wendy back into focus.

"And here I thought you had natural red hair," Nash said. He nudged her behind a knee with the beer bottle, causing her to yelp.

"It's naturally *reddish*," she said. "It just needs a little help to reach its full potential."

"That smell is overpowering," Nash said. He walked to the bathroom window and breathed in some fresh air—at least what passed for fresh in San Bernardino. "What you women will do for beauty."

"Be quiet. I've only got to leave it in twenty more minutes. It won't kill you."

He stood at the window a moment longer, sucking in air and surveying the parking lot, empty of people but still bathed in light from the sodium vapor lamps. One cast a stage-worthy spot on the Dumpsters at the far edge of the blacktop. As he caught another whiff of hair-dye ammonia, Nash found himself similarly illuminated.

"Thanks," he said, turning back to her. "You just gave me an idea to go with my headache."

"How's that?" Wendy asked as she wiped the dye off her ears with a damp cloth.

"The family they found dead the other day in the supermarket Dumpster."

"Yeah?"

"Their deaths might be tied into the story I'm working on."

"The one you got suspended over?"

"The very same." He took a deep breath. "The piece we ran about the family mentioned that they might have been asphyxiated. And this ammonia smell—along with your comment—got me to thinking about what might have done them in. They were found near the drive-in, but there are several factories in the area as well. Whoever killed them might work at one."

"So I gave you a clue?" Wendy seemed delighted.

"We like to call them story leads." Nash smiled. "But, yeah, you did."

Chapter Sixteen

Over coffee in the *Ledger*'s break room late Thursday morning, Nash and Escobar shared what they'd turned up on Carr. After leaving Wendy's apartment literally red-handed—he'd accidentally run his fingers through her damp hair while kissing her goodnight—Nash had gone home and studied the police reports again.

Carr and Reese Stevens had been business partners in the late fifties. The first of Carr's several minor run-ins with the law was written up in a report dated April 12, 1958. Carr and Stevens were engaged in "a major altercation" in front of a car dealership they owned when a squad car arrived on the scene. No charges had been filed and the matter, apparently, was dropped.

"I got something even better," Escobar said. "Klete wasn't in the mood to do me any favors today, so I asked a P.I. I know to run a search on Malcolm Snipes through the National Criminal Information Center." He paused, tapping his notebook. "You were right, this guy is a pro fruitcase. If Snipes isn't on the FBI Top Ten, he at least gets honorable mention."

The search of the nation's police records had turned up three prior felony convictions and eight outstanding warrants on Snipes. He had served seventeen years in various correctional institutions for manslaughter, gunrunning, kidnapping, and polygamy. He was still wanted for two counts of

witness tampering, three other weapons charges, intimida-
tion of a federal officer, burglary, and assault. The feds had
traced him for several years as he moved throughout the
Southwest under seven known aliases.

At every stop, Snipes had set up a pseudo-religious paramilitary survivalist group. Since his last release from prison in
1995, he had managed to stay ahead of the law. Two years
ago, they had lost track of him completely.

"The same year Evan Carr renovated the drive-ins," Nash
said. After hearing the laundry list on Snipes, he felt damn
lucky to be alive.

"And that's also when Reese Stevens lost his bid for the
mayor's seat," Escobar said. "I haven't been this excited
since I found the sheriff in bed with a hooker last year."

Nash was wired as well. Something in the predatory nature of the species gave him and all the other reporters he
knew an incredible adrenaline high every time they were
about to tear down the walls of somebody's fortress. He took
a sip of coffee and grinned at Escobar. "So where do we go
next?"

"I'll check out the zoning on the drive-ins and see if
they're restrictive enough to give Carr a motive for secrecy.
You can't just buy a city inspector now like in the corrupt old
days, so major violations can mean tens of thousands in
fines," Escobar said. "And if the work is exposed before he's
able to get a high-rise exemption for the site, he might have to
scuttle the whole deal. I think it's time you paid a visit to
Spice Warren's construction outfit to see if you can find out
exactly what kind of 'renovation' job he actually did on those
drive-ins."

"One other thing," Nash said. "Is there any way you might
be able to find out what killed that family in the Von's Dumpster?"

"I know a guy in the medical examiner's office who might provide some off-the-record help."

"Thanks. Meet you back here at three?" Nash asked as he gulped the last of his coffee.

"You know it, Rambler."

As Nash drove the twenty miles west to Rancho Cucamonga, he thought through the other key information he'd turned up in the police reports. The dead family in the Von's Dumpster had last been seen heading to church last Thursday evening, according to neighbors.

The only interesting new detail on the Shane Littlefeather murder was the fact that the three kill shots had been fired at a range of 325 yards. Nash wondered if there were any marksmanship medals pinned to the skeletons in Malcolm Snipes' closet.

The file on the trap incident at the Star-Time was brief. Just as Carr had told Nash on the phone, he'd stepped forward to take responsibility for the "bizarre incident" on his property. No charges had yet been filed, because the police were still looking for a suspect. The report listed one "Steve Malcolm" as the drive-in manager. Make that eight known aliases on Snipes, Nash thought.

The report also noted that the bear trap was made in 1853, in French Canadian territory. Said property would be remanded to Evan Carr to be washed and placed back in his collector's case at the close of the investigation.

Nash pulled into the deserted parking lot of Warren Construction and had a quick look around the grounds before heading into the office. Next to a gravel lot filled with dump trucks, front-end loaders, cranes, and fork-lifts sat an enormous aluminum shed holding bags of cement, steel girders, and the like. Definitely a large-job operation, Nash thought as he opened the door of the small office at the front of the parking lot.

Obviously meant to function rather than impress, the suite was graced with heavily stained indoor-outdoor carpeting, an open bullpen area for mid-level staff, four offices spaced evenly around the perimeter, and a secretary's station ringed with ancient filing cabinets that blocked access to the floor from the reception area.

Nash walked up to the secretary, who was writing on two files with one hand and cradling the receiver of a black phone in the other.

"Hang on a sec," she told the caller when she noticed Nash standing at the desk. "Sorry," she said to him pleasantly, "you just missed everybody. They're all over to Palm Springs for the groundbreaking of the Sea Breeze Mall."

"Maybe you can help me," Nash said.

"Maybe so," she said, smiling. "Excuse me a moment." She took her caller off hold and promised to call right back. "What do you need? Brochure? Or are you here to drop off a contract or something?"

"Actually, I'm from the *Ledger.* My name's Nashua Hansen and—"

"We've already got a subscription," she said, picking up the phone without looking at it.

"I'm not a salesman," he said.

She re-hooked the receiver and waited.

"I'm here to do a feature for our annual progress edition on the major projects you've completed in the last year."

"Isn't that nice. Tell you what, Mr. Nashua Hansen, Mr. Warren will be back in the office on Monday. I bet he'd have some time to talk with you in the afternoon."

"That'd be great. I'm sorry, I didn't get your name."

"Sandy," she said, holding out her hand. "Pleased to make your acquaintance."

"Listen, Sandy, I don't mean to bug you with this, but there's another story I'm working on that involves Warren Construction." He told her about the feature on Carr's drive-ins. "The story's due tomorrow morning and I've got just about all the information I need, except some of the construction specifics. How much concrete was poured for the new snack bars, that type of thing."

"I can't let you see the dollar figures on the contracts," she said. "But if you tell me exactly what you need by way of the other numbers, I'll look them up for you."

Almost as soon as Sandy began reading the CarrCorp. file, she stopped.

"This work summary must be from another job," she said.

"What do you mean?" Nash asked.

"According to this, we hauled enough dirt and poured enough concrete to build a parking garage. I've just got to get this mixed-up filing system in shape."

When Nash got back to the office, he made a beeline for Escobar. Although the coroner's inquest was still in progress, Curt's source confirmed that the examiner had found traces of hydrogen selenide in the lungs of the mother, the father, and their six-year-old girl. The gas, deadly if inhaled, was used in high-tech manufacturing. There were still no suspects in the killings. Nash made a mental note to talk with the neighbors—and to check and see if any local factory was missing a canister of lethal gas.

Meanwhile, Escobar's trip to City Hall revealed that none of Carr's three drive-in properties were zoned for commercial structures of more than two stories.

"But if he put a parking garage under each theater, he

could be thinking high-rise," Escobar said. "What are you laughing at?"

"Has anybody ever told you olive pants do not go terribly well with a charcoal sport coat?"

"I'm behind in the laundry." Escobar tore open another package of Twinkies. "Plus, I'm putting on some extra weight. Half my pants are too tight."

"Must be stress," Nash said, grabbing one of the yellow cakes.

"Must be." Escobar held up his right index finger. It was covered with excess Twinkie goo he had wiped off the waxed paper tray. "I think maybe Carr figured Reese Stevens would push through the necessary zoning changes when he was elected mayor." He paused to lick the cream filling off his digit. "Then, when he lost, Carr decided to just sit on the property until the political climate was right."

"I still don't see why he'd bring somebody like Malcolm Snipes in on the project."

"That is a sticky one. Maybe we're going at this from the wrong angle. What if Snipes is using the garages for a meth lab or something?"

"That would explain why he was so upset to see me snooping around," Nash agreed. "But it doesn't figure that Carr would pay for heavy construction like that just so some loony tune could keep the neighborhood flying."

"Maybe not," Escobar said. "But we're not going to find out sitting here with our thumbs up our collective ass. I think we need to make a run to the 7-Eleven."

"What for?"

"To stock up on junk food for our stakeout." Escobar missed the trash can with the Twinkie wrapper by a good three feet.

★ ★ ★ ★ ★

They had decided to stake out two of the three drive-ins until nine the following morning, a Friday. Figuring that Malcolm Snipes would recognize Nash and his car, Escobar took the Star-Time while Nash watched the Twi-Nite across town.

"I thought I had some action when a van stopped outside the theater after the show, but it was just some kid getting sick," Escobar said as he poured two extra-large coffees. "I did hear a stinky double-feature on the radio, though."

"That's more exciting than my night," Nash said. It was nine-thirty A.M. and neither of them had stopped home for a change of clothes. They both needed showers, Nash thought as he slugged down his coffee; it was getting pretty close in the break room.

"Let's talk while we walk," Escobar said. "If I don't get some fresh air soon, I'm going to keel over."

Downtown San Bernardino was not the stuff of promotional posters. As Nash and Escobar walked past the bleak collection of office buildings and parking garages on D Street, they came across only late commuters rushing to work and several transients who were opening their eyes on another lousy day in the shadowy alcoves they called home. Hanging a left, they strolled past the three-for-a-buck movie house and a local porno palace. "Kit Kat Presents *Sperminator III* Plus Two Classic Shorts," the marquee read. "All Film, No Video. Finest Quality." Nash couldn't imagine moving to this city by choice.

"I say we go home, get some rest, and then continue the stakeout at two or three this afternoon," Escobar said. "Something's bound to turn up."

"I've been thinking about that security check you ran on

Snipes," Nash said. "Maybe it's time to tip the feds."

"All in good time, Rambler. Remember how they fucked up that Reese Stevens investigation? You want to bring somebody down right, you do it yourself. If we drop the dime on Snipes now, Evan Carr walks away clean."

"Okay, but don't get careless around the Star-Time. If we go in, we should do it together."

"Don't worry about me," Escobar said, stopping to pull up his left pant leg just enough to reveal a snub-nosed .38 Special snapped into an ankle holster. "I've got all my bases covered."

After he showered and changed, Nash turned on a rerun of the original "Bob Newhart Show," his favorite sitcom. He needed a half-hour of Dr. Hartley to help him forget about the damned investigation for a while. Homer walked in as the theme music was ending.

"This is a classic," he said, plopping onto the couch.

"You like Bob Newhart?" Nash was surprised. Bob's humor seemed a little subtle for a man who thought detailing cars was a prime career opportunity.

"Oh, sure, it's a funny show," Homer said. "But the best thing to do is watch it with a bunch of buddies and a keg of beer. Whenever somebody says, 'Hi, Bob,' you have to pound one back. You're laughing at everything on the screen inside of ten minutes. Which reminds me."

"Grab me one, too," Nash said as Homer opened the refrigerator for a Pabst. The twelve-pack lasted through a "Cheers" repeat and "Jeopardy!" Nash hurt Homer's feelings by laughing after Homer missed every answer in Double Jeopardy.

"I still think Velveeta is the most popular cheese in France," he said testily. "Everyone I know eats it."

"Exactly how many Frenchmen do you party with in a given week?" Nash asked.

"Fuckin' frogs," Homer muttered to himself. "I'm going out for more beer."

The alcohol made Nash even more drowsy than he had been when he walked in the door, but he decided to call Wendy before taking a nap.

"Hello?" said the man on the other end of the line.

"I'm sorry," Nash said. "Wrong number." He dialed again, carefully.

"Yeah?" It was the same guy.

"Uh, is Wendy there?" He didn't know what else to say.

"No, she's at the store." The man didn't seem eager to continue the conversation.

"Who's this?" Nash asked.

"Who the hell is this?" the man said.

A real people person. "My name's Nash. And you are?"

"I'm Bill. Listen, is this about work?"

"Yes, yes it is." Think quickly, Nash told himself. "I'm verifying the schedule for next week. Could you have her give me a call when she gets back?"

Bill grunted in the affirmative and hung up. Nash lay on his bed wondering how long Wendy had known her boyfriend was coming home on leave. Maybe it was time to wrap this whole mess up and get out of town, he thought as he closed his eyes for twelve hours of restless sleep.

Chapter Seventeen

Jogging across the Cal State San Bernardino campus from Devil Creek Levee to the dorms on North Park Boulevard, Nash wondered if he should write Wendy off or fight for her. She hadn't returned his call last night. Maybe she didn't have a chance. His life was turning into a soap opera, and he had the feeling it was in danger of being canceled for a mid-season replacement.

He tried calling Escobar from the nearly deserted student union for an update, but there was no answer at his apartment or at the office. Probably out treating himself to a big meal. Nash felt guilty for not watching the Twi-Nite, but at least now he was fresh enough to do a full Saturday's work on the investigation. He decided to start by talking with the neighbors of the dead family from the supermarket Dumpster.

The family had lived in a trailer park in Rialto, a working-class suburb of row houses and factories that began at the west edge of the city. Nash could tell by the peeling paint on the warped speed-limit sign out front that the park had been around since before the advent of the double-wide. He parked the 2002 next to a pale green single with a police notice tacked to the door and scanned the neighboring yards for signs of life.

Trailer parks were as bad as college campuses when it

came to activity on a Saturday morning. Nash mounted the cinderblock steps of a relatively new brown double-wide. A barking dog was tied to a long lead in the backyard. Nash paused for a moment straining to hear signs of life. Was that a TV playing in the distance? When he knocked on the door, the dog stopped barking and ran around the side of the trailer to see what was up. She was a good-looking golden retriever. Probably trained to chase ducks. Or wild geese. He knocked again, louder this time.

"Hold your friggin' horses," a man yelled from the rear of the trailer. "I'm on the pot."

Nash walked over to get a closer look at the retriever. As he approached, the dog began to whimper and jerk wildly on the rope tied to its collar.

"Hey there, pretty one," Nash said, holding out his right hand, palm up, for inspection. The retriever brought her nose up close and snuffled around the hand for a moment, then stuck out her tongue and began licking his palm.

"That's my girl." He scratched her behind the ears. "You look like you need a good run." As the last word left Nash's lips, the dog looked up at him with joyful expectation; from the looks of the torn-up sod in the back yard, it had been a long time since she'd been off her leash.

As Nash bent down to give her a good pet, the man of the house opened the door and jumped down off the steps.

"Simmer down there, Angie," he said, wiping his damp hands on the front of a clean white T-shirt. "Sorry about the de-lay," he said with a pronounced backwoods twang. Hard-scrabble handsome in the tradition of a middle-aged Steve McQueen, the man sported bushy brown sideburns that ended a few inches from the tip of a clean-shaven chin. "I see you've already made friends with Angie," he said, leaning over to give the retriever's ears a playful tug.

"You take her hunting?" Nash asked.

"Used to take her out flushing quail in the Appalachians, but she's pretty much a city dog now." He stood up and held out his hand. "I'm Wayne Easler."

Nash introduced himself and told the man he was doing a follow-up report on the death of his neighbors for the *Ledger*.

"Oh yeah," Wayne said, shaking his head. He shot a glance at the empty trailer next door and squinted his eyes as if trying to remember an important detail. He looked back at Nash and held out his palms. "Not much to say, really. The Millers was pretty good friends of mine the past couple years." He paused and took a longer look at the trailer. "I guess you'd say we were more good neighbors than friends. You know, trading tools, drinking a beer in front of a game on the weekends. Their kid Sarah used to take old Angie out for a walk every day after school." He turned away and took a deep breath. His corded neck muscles were visibly tense.

"Why don't you come inside and have a sit," Wayne said over his shoulder. When the man turned around, Nash saw that he was close to tears.

Nash was surprised at how clean the trailer was inside. Except for a car magazine and a stack of plastic drink coasters, the oak coffee table was bare, as was the bar separating the small kitchen from the living room. A poster of Elvis in Hawaii, hanging in a place of honor over an ancient rack stereo system complete with turntable, was the only artwork in evidence. Although Wayne had not yet entered the realm of CD players, a Bearcat police scanner sat atop a twenty-nine-inch Sony Wega with remote control.

"I heard the first reports on that." Wayne nodded toward the Bearcat as he brought a Bud long-neck over to the black vinyl couch where Nash was sitting. "I sat by the scanner for hours after they discovered the bodies. I had just seen 'em the day before, all dressed up, going to that new church of theirs. When the police said the little girl was holding a stuffed tiger, I started feeling sick. I'd just won one for Sarah at the fair. When they didn't come home, I knew it was them."

"I'm sorry for your loss," Nash said.

"Hell," Wayne said, "you don't know the half of it." He took a long pull from his beer and stood up. "Can I tell you something off the record?"

"Whatever you're comfortable with."

Wayne picked up a photo of a winsome blond woman from the telephone stand next to the couch and handed it to Nash. She was standing in front of a cabin in the mountains with her right hip thrust out and her hands crossed high on her chest. It was a defiant pose and there was pleasure evident in her smile, but Nash caught a glimpse of guilt in the woman's eyes.

"I guess it don't matter much now," Wayne said. "I figured it would be okay to put her picture out since they're all gone. Janie told me she'd be leaving Pete soon as Sarah went into high school in a few years. She didn't want her growing up in a broken home and all. Seems like Janie was always thinking of everyone but herself. That was a big part of her appeal." Wayne's voice broke on the last part.

Nash waited until he regained his composure to ask, "Did she ever mention anything funny about this new church?"

"Shit yes," Wayne said, plopping back down in his easy chair. "It was Pete got all mixed up in that end-of-the-world crap. I'm telling you, they were scared, Janie and Sarah both. Crazy preacher showing off the guns he'd bought with last week's collection, survival weekends out in the desert. I told her to try and talk some sense into Pete, and they had some horrible fights over it. Couple of times, Sarah snuck over here and slept on the couch with Angie. It tears me up just to think about it."

"Do you think the church had something to do with their deaths?"

"Who else?" Wayne fixed Nash with a hard gaze.

"Why didn't you tell the police?"

"I did." Wayne slammed the beer bottle on the coffee table, causing a pillar of foam to crawl out of the neck. "But I didn't know the name of the church or where it was. Janie said it was some big secret and Pete would kill her if she told anybody. I think she was afraid I'd do something foolish like go down and bust the place up." He clenched his fists. "I probably would have, too."

"Did Janie give you any specifics?"

"They'd been going every Thursday for about two months." Wayne rolled his eyes up. "I think she mentioned the preacher's name once or twice."

Nash wondered what alias Malcolm Snipes was using in front of his flock this time.

"Wait. I got it," Wayne said, snapping his fingers. "Janie said his name was Reverend Stevens."

Chapter Eighteen

Where the hell was Curt? Nash cradled the receiver at the gas station pay phone. He didn't want to seem paranoid, but after what Malcolm Snipes had done to his wrist, he decided to drive by the Star-Time, just in case Escobar had wandered into a sucker punch.

As he drove, Nash went over the who, what, where, when, why, and how of the Evan Carr story. Wayne had taken him a giant step closer to confirming the who, what, and how: Reese Stevens and Malcolm Snipes were running some type of survivalist church, with Spice Warren and Evan Carr contributing the location and the cash. After hearing the information from the Warren Construction files, he was pretty sure the where was a parking garage underneath one of the drive-ins: Instead of meth, Snipes was selling salvation. As for when, the whole scheme was probably set up as early as three years back, when Stevens was running hard for the mayor's seat. That left only the all-important why.

Why would Evan Carr, a sharp operator who could probably turn a profit selling Cadillacs in Japan, get involved with such a risky operation? Nash couldn't see how Carr would expect to gain anything beyond a minimal kickback from collection-plate revenues. Maybe his old business partner Stevens had forced Carr into the deal by threatening to release some type of incriminating evidence.

And then there was the death of Warren's construction supervisor, Shane Littlefeather. He might have overheard the wrong conversation and then threatened to upset the apple cart if Carr and Warren wouldn't let him in on the action. The threat of exposure might have led Snipes or Stevens to kill the Miller family as well. But why with poison gas? That wasn't the usual method of execution for a heavily armed group of survivalists.

Still too many weak links to drop the dime on Carr, Nash decided as the Star-Time came into view. He let out a relieved sigh when he saw Escobar's convertible parked across the street from the theater. Nash couldn't believe the guy was still on the job; no wonder he had won so many reporting awards.

But when Nash pulled up alongside the Skylark, he saw that the car was empty. He parked the 2002 and jogged around to peer through Escobar's window. There was a sheet of white paper sitting on the leather seat. He looked around for signs of a set-up, then opened the door and grabbed the note.

"He's not dead yet," it read. "But he will be if you're still in town tomorrow. If you tell the police, we will know."

Nash jumped into the BMW and left it in first gear, peeling out and picking up speed until the whine of the engine hurt his ears. Downshifting hard, he topped sixty down the industrial parkway, desperate to get to the Von's supermarket and scared of what he might find waiting for him there. When he opened the lid of the Dumpster, the stench of rotten vegetables nearly knocked him off his feet, but there were no bodies hidden in the mounds of cabbage.

When Homer walked into the apartment a few hours later, Nash was almost finished packing.

"What the hell?" Homer asked. He picked up a glass Nash had just dropped into a carton and set it back on the counter. "Was it something I said?"

"They got Escobar," Nash said. "I don't have time to give you the whole story, but the bottom line is, they threatened to kill him if I don't get out of Dodge by sundown."

"You're just going to run away?"

"That's what I want them to think." Nash paused to wipe the sweat from his forehead with a paper towel. "I'm checking into a Motel 6 just past Redlands. Then I'm going over to L.A. to drop off the 2002 and pick up a rental car. I think I can stay under cover and crack this thing in a couple of days. If Escobar's not out by then, I'm calling in the feds."

"Why not bring in the locals?"

"Curt busted eight cops on theft charges a few years back. If I called in a missing person's report, I'm sure Evan Carr would hear about it."

"Can I help?" Homer was clearly excited at the prospect of action.

"I thought you'd never ask," Nash said, throwing a duffel bag onto his small pile of possessions. "First off, if Wendy calls, tell her I got fired from the paper and left in a snit. The less she knows, the safer she is. And if the paper calls, tell them you don't know where I am."

"But what can I *do?*" Homer pleaded.

"If things get tight, I might need your help finding Curt. And there is one other thing."

"Name it, man."

"I need you to get me a gun."

"No problem. Meet me at the detail shop tomorrow morning at eight. I'll be waiting for you in the parking lot around back."

"Now help me carry this shit down to the car," Nash said, grabbing a box. "I've got a lot of work ahead of me this afternoon."

The *Ledger*'s morgue was as empty on Saturday as it was during the week, Nash thought as he pulled out the file on environmental hazards. On his second time through, he found the article he was looking for, dated two months back: "Missing cylinder holds deadly gas." The first few paragraphs of the story were enough to send his pulse into overdrive:

> "A cylinder of gas capable of killing everyone within a three-quarter-mile radius was reported stolen from a Rancho Cucamonga gas supplier Tuesday night.
>
> "The sheriff's department believes the thief stole the aluminum cylinder to sell for scrap and may be unaware it is filled with potentially lethal hydrogen selenide, said Sheriff's Lt. David Vinson.
>
> "The flammable, colorless gas is two times heavier than air. If released, it would travel near the ground and a 10- to 12-knot wind could spread lethal gas up to three quarters of a mile, according to the county department of environmental health services.
>
> "The gas, which affects the lungs, liver, and spleen, can be fatal if inhaled, swallowed, or absorbed through the skin or eyes, Vinson said. If released, the eight pounds of gas in the cylinder could kill 'every living soul in the exposed area,' and could remain in lethal concentrations for a half-hour or more, he added."

Nash ripped the article off its cardboard backing and sprinted down the hall to his cubicle. The man who answered the phone at the gas supplier seemed willing to help, but didn't have much information to offer. They'd never recovered the hydrogen selenide, and the sheriff's department still had no suspects. At least now Nash knew where the Miller family's killer—or killers—had picked up their murder weapon.

"One last question," he said.

"Sure," the man replied.

"Have you ever supplied gas to Warren Construction?"

There was a pause, and then the sound of computer keys being punched. "They're not on record as a customer," he said finally. "But it wouldn't surprise me if they were."

"Why's that?" Nash asked.

"Well, their office is only two blocks away."

The tumblers were beginning to fall into place, Nash thought, but he still couldn't open the lock on this story. He grabbed a phone book and found the phone number and address of Shane Littlefeather's family and of Trudy Waylin, the high school girl who was working at the drive-in the night Nash found Ronald Slasnik in the trap.

He booted up his computer and dashed off an e-mail to Escobar. If Carr bought the disappearing act and released Escobar, this message would bring him up to date.

Then, Nash hammered out a note to Lydia, the final element of his plan to throw Carr off the scent.

"Thanks for nothing, bitch," the first line read.

Ah, that has a nice ring to it, he thought.

"You ruin my career and then expect me to sit around writing headlines for eight weeks? Get real, get a life, and get out of my face. Sincerely, Nashua Hansen."

When she saw that on Monday, she was sure to phone Carr and tell him she'd fired Nash right after Carr had lodged his complaint. Which reminded him, he had a few calls to make himself.

Slow as ever, Slant Williams answered the phone on the seventh ring.

"Yes?" he said mildly.

"Slant, it's Nash Hansen."

"I thought I told you not to bother me."

Nash couldn't help smiling. "You also said I should get my nose bloody. I'm working on a real gusher right now."

"What do you want me to do about it?" Slant's voice had risen just enough to betray his interest.

"First thing Monday morning you're going to receive a call from either the assistant city editor or the publisher demanding that I be immediately brought back to school and suspended."

"What?" It was the first time Nash had heard Slant yell.

"Trust me on this. Will you do that?"

"Just tell me what you want me to do," his adviser replied, regaining his composure.

"Stall them, commiserate with them, whatever you have to do to hold up the process for a couple of days."

"What then?"

"Do you have any friends at the *L.A. Times*?"

"No, I don't think so. I know the managing editor of the *Orange County Register* pretty well, though."

"Great. The next time I call, I'll be finishing up the most sensational story to hit Southern California since the riots."

"I'll be standing by," Slant said.

Nash found Carl Barns in the photographers' hovel at the opposite end of the newsroom, checking the dot pattern on several shots he had taken of the space shuttle landing in the Mojave desert earlier that morning.

"The Edwards Air Force goons had us a mile away from the runway, and they told us to be thankful we weren't in the distant viewing area!" Carl said, holding up a brilliant black-

and-white photo of the Columbia, its nose pointing slightly upward as it prepared to touch down. Nash could even make out wisps of smoke coming off the blackened heat tiles on the shuttle's underbelly.

"How'd you get a print that clear?" Nash asked.

"I used a five-hundred millimeter lens with a doubler on it. Even so, what you see here was only about a quarter of the original frame. Had to use a heavy-duty tripod and remote shutter release to get a steady shot, of course."

"Are you off tomorrow?"

"Sure. Why?"

"It's time to shoot some folks in mid-felony."

Nash told the photographer his theory about the underground bunker, the survivalist church, and his run-in with Malcolm Snipes, but he held back the information about Escobar.

"I want you on the top of the tallest building you can find overlooking the Star-Time tomorrow morning," Nash continued. "But stay at least two blocks away. If Snipes sees you, I guarantee you'll regret it."

"What am I looking for?" Carl asked.

"Any sign of activity, license plates, faces. Try to pinpoint the entrance to the bunker. Take as much film as you can carry."

"When do you need the contact sheets?"

"Immediately." Nash handed Carl a slip of paper with the address of a local gas station written on it. "Be at the pay phone there at ten A.M. Monday. I'll call you for a report."

"Carr's gunning for you hard," Carl said, frowning.

Nash nodded. "It's important that no one else know about any of this until we nail him."

"My shutter is closed," Carl said, stuffing the slip of paper into one of the hundred tiny pockets on his vest.

★ ★ ★ ★ ★

Before leaving the paper, Nash photocopied his notes from the investigation and dropped them in the Federal Express box for Monday delivery. If he was killed, at least the package would give Slant enough information to go to the police.

Nash took a deep breath. He had set into motion a series of events which would lead either to the downfall of a group of men implicated in at least four murders, or to the death of Curt Escobar. And now he was in danger as well. The inevitability of it all made him feel strangely calm and confident.

Halfway to L.A., the music began to come alive in Nash's head once again. As he sang "Brown Eyed Girl," he rolled down the window and started tapping out a syncopated beat with his cast on the front door of the 2002.

Chapter Nineteen

In his dream that night, Wendy and Curt Escobar were making love on a blanket in the middle of a construction site. Nash watched with envy as Wendy dug her toes into the soft, recently excavated earth while Escobar moved violently on top of her. In the distance, he could hear a group of people chanting in prayer and asking to be healed. He wanted them to be quiet so he could make out the name Wendy was saying over and over as she dug her fingernails into Escobar's shoulder blades. He yelled at them, but they would not shut up.

He looked down at the gun in his right hand and pointed it at the group of churchgoers. He kept squeezing the trigger until they all lay bleeding and silent, but he still could not hear the name Wendy was calling out.

In a fury, Nash pulled Escobar off of her. His face was pale and there was a small, black bullet hole in the middle of his forehead. Wendy lay there naked, her legs spread wide and her breasts shaking as she began to laugh.

It's too late, lover, she said to him. You've already lost us both.

Chapter Twenty

It didn't seem like a Sunday morning. The parkway next to the Motel 6 was nearly bumper to bumper when Nash checked out at seven and climbed into the rented brown Oldsmobile. The pace of life never slowed in Southern California. The stores were always open, the treadmills at the health clubs never stopped, and violent death was a daily occurrence.

He didn't have time to relax, anyway. He checked his new San Diego Padres cap and sunglasses in the rearview. If he couldn't call in the cavalry for Escobar just yet, he could at least flesh out the story with a few background interviews.

When Nash pulled into the back parking lot of the detail shop, Homer drew down on him with a pistol that looked large even in his meaty hands.

"Whoa," Nash said, pointing an index finger at Homer out the open car window.

"You can never be too safe," Homer said, easing the hammer down. "Somebody tore up the apartment pretty good last night when I was out getting this."

"I'm glad you weren't around. Did you make sure you weren't followed this morning?"

Homer grinned. "Sure did, boss. I walked through about a mile of yards and back alleys before I doubled back here."

"You might want to think about blowing town, too, before

this gets ugly," Nash said, hefting the gun in his right hand.

"Are you kidding? I'm just starting to get interested." Homer paused. "I saw Wendy this morning."

"What did she say?" Nash tried not to sound too interested.

"Just hello to me. She was with that Army guy. I think they were on their way out to breakfast; they were carrying a Sunday paper."

"Did she look happy?" He had to ask.

"Hard to tell. She kind of avoided looking me in the eye."

"So, what type of hardware is this?" Nash pointed the big revolver at the side of the building. He held his arm out straight and squinted his left eye in classic Clint Eastwood style. The gun was much heavier than he'd expected.

"That's a .44 Magnum Ruger Redhawk," Homer said quietly. "It holds six rounds and will kill pretty much anything you point it at." He showed Nash how to load it and hold it properly in both hands and told him to exhale gently before squeezing the trigger. "And if you start shooting at somebody, don't stop until the gun is empty."

Nash shuddered as he remembered last night's dream. "You must have done a lot of shooting."

"Naw, I just seen this stuff in the movies," Homer replied. "It all makes good sense to me, though."

"Thanks, that makes me feel a hell of a lot better." Nash looked down at the gun in his hand, and, for a moment, decided to give it back to Homer. But the feeling passed and he found himself running an index finger along the dull blue metal of the five-inch barrel instead. It felt like power, he thought as he traced the outline of the round opening. His hand began to sweat as he squeezed the grip. This would allow him to channel his anger into action. He could go to the drive-in right now and punch Malcolm Snipes' ticket for the final feature; he wouldn't even have time to buy popcorn.

It was a tempting notion, but Nash squelched his desire for vigilante justice by reminding himself that the .38 Special strapped to Escobar's ankle obviously hadn't been of much use when he was ambushed at the stakeout Friday night. Better to stick with what you know, he thought, and save the firepower for an emergency.

Nash opened the passenger door of the Olds and stashed the .44 and a box of shells in the glove compartment. "You're going to stick around?" he asked.

Homer nodded.

"Then be ready to back me up when I call you."

"Count on it." Homer held out his hand.

When Nash shook it, something poked his palm. It was a small wooden sculpture of a wolf, sitting on its haunches, ready to howl.

"A guy sold it to me when we stopped for gas on the way through Nevada," Homer said. "Supposed to be real heavy medicine."

"Uh huh. How much did it cost?"

"Two bucks," Homer said sheepishly. "But I figured it couldn't hurt."

Trudy Waylin's house was on the north side of town. It was a quintessential California ranch–style number, low and long and painted a pale peach. Instead of a lush lawn, however, the house was fronted by a faux-desert tableau. Two cacti, a yucca tree, and a Conestoga wheel planted in a pebble garden evoked Western film sets of the 1920s. Nash was sure that wasn't the intended effect, but he found the view perversely pleasing. The only thing missing was a bleached cow skull atop the mailbox.

It was early yet for a Sunday, ten-thirty, but Nash had a

hunch there were no slug-a-beds living in this house. Even though there was a doorbell and a small brass knocker provided, Nash rapped on the front door with his knuckles. It sounded more official, he thought.

The insistent voice of a little boy came from the direction of the living room. "Trudy, someone's at the door."

"I heard it, Ryan." Trudy Waylin's voice came from what might have been the kitchen.

"Hurry and bring my Cocoa Puffs before they get all soggy," the boy hollered.

"Hold your horses, you little brat," she said as she opened the door.

"Hi, Trudy," Nash said. When he smiled at her, the bridge of her nose pinkened slightly and she looked at the ground.

"Nash Hansen," she said. "I never thought I'd see you again. I liked the story you wrote about that guy in the trap."

She was smiling expectantly, as if waiting for him to hand her a prize envelope. She looked to be about seventeen, a junior or senior in high school. Laid-back fashionable in a white cotton jumper over a pink T-shirt. Her black hair was cut into a loose pageboy. Call me in three years, he thought.

"Look, would you like to come inside?" she asked.

"You got any Cocoa Puffs left?"

"No!" cried the little boy, who had taken up a hiding place behind the door.

"Oh, Ryan, he was just teasing," Trudy said as she squatted down with her arms open. The boy, a healthy-looking five-year-old, shot out from behind the door with such startling velocity that he almost knocked Trudy over when he leapt into her grasp.

"Nash, meet my little brother, king of the Cocoa Puffs." By this time, Ryan had buried his head against his sister's shoulder. "Don't be afraid, big guy. Nash is a reporter from the newspaper," she whispered in his ear.

"Mommy said no boys in the house," Ryan replied.

"Oh hush," Trudy said. "I think I hear your cereal getting soggy." At that, Ryan wriggled free and disappeared into the kitchen.

"My parents are at a horse breeders' convention in San Diego," Trudy said as she poured two Diet Cokes into highball glasses. "They own a stable near Redlands."

"I hear it's nice out that way," Nash said.

"You mean you work at the *Ledger* and you've never even been to Redlands?"

He explained about the internship and asked her how things were at the Star-Time.

"How should I know? I quit the day after that guy almost lost his foot." She took a long pull from her Diet Coke and then rested her elbows on the dining-room table. "Weird stuff like that happened almost every day I worked there. It creeped me out."

"What kind of stuff?"

"What kind of story are you writing?"

"Just a follow-up on what happened to Ronald Slasnik."

"Who?" she asked. "Oh, the guy in the trap. I never saw him again."

Nash nodded and started jotting down notes. Trudy craned her neck slightly to see what he was writing, but Nash held the pad close to his chest.

"You were going to tell me about some strange occurrences at the Star-Time?"

Trudy Waylin settled back into her chair and considered the question. "The biggest thing I couldn't figure out was why Mr. Carr never fired Malcolm," she said, spitting out the manager's name. "He was always yelling at Mr. Carr on the phone, telling him to get off his back, making all sorts of threats. It didn't make any sense."

"What kind of threats?"

"Just general stuff, like 'I'll ruin you,' that type of thing. Malcolm Snipes was a creep."

"Did he bother you?"

"He wasn't that kind of creep." She leaned forward again. "Malcolm was just plain mean. And he had all kinds of stupid rules."

"Like?"

"Like we couldn't come to work before six P.M. on Sunday and none of us were allowed in the storage cellar."

"What storage cellar?"

"There's this trap door in Malcolm's office that he keeps padlocked. All the supplies are down there."

"And you never saw inside?"

"Nope," she said. "If we needed anything we had to tell Malcolm. A few times we ran out of stuff like cups and popcorn when he was gone, but that was just too bad for us. I think he keeps dirty magazines down there or something." The pink color returned to Trudy's nose as she said it, but this time she controlled her embarrassment enough to maintain eye contact.

"Were there any other strange things going on at the Star-Time when you worked there?" Nash asked. Trudy's co-quettish manner seemed to indicate that she had thought of him a few times after their first meeting. He was flattered, and a little amused.

As if she were reading his thoughts, her blush deepened considerably.

"I'm such a spaz," she said quietly.

"Not at all," Nash said. "Relax. A lot of people are nervous when they're being interviewed."

"It's just, well, your story made me feel like kind of a hero."

"I think you were a hero that night, calling the paramedics so fast and helping to stop the blood. A lot of people would have frozen up."

"Thanks," she said, smiling as her blush receded. "Now where were we? Weird stuff, right? Well, one day I walked in and Malcolm was moving this silver canister into the storage room. You know, like a gas canister with valves on top?"

"Did you ask what it was?"

"That's just it," Trudy said. "He told me it was helium for some promotional balloons. But he never talked about it again after that and I never saw any balloons."

"Anything else?"

"One more thing about the trap," she said. "Malcolm called Mr. Carr the next day. I overheard the conversation because Malcolm was yelling so loud. He said something about how Mr. Carr had made his point and he'd get his god-damn money. It was real heated."

Nash polished off his Diet Coke and stood up.

"Trudy, you have no idea what a hero you are today." He leaned forward to kiss her on the forehead just as Ryan walked in from the kitchen carefully holding his half-empty cereal bowl.

"Yuck," he said, adding, "Can I have some more Puffs to finish my milk?"

Chapter Twenty-one

Shane Littlefeather's wife lived in a luxury Victorville condominium near the Southern California Logistics Airport, formerly George Air Force Base. From the end of her block, Nash watched a huge transport lumber down the ten-thousand-foot runway. Even at a distance of several hundred yards, the noise was overpowering.

At the entrance of the three-story, white stucco building, Nash pushed the buzzer for number 206. Through the glass security door, he could see palm trees and a swimming pool in the condo's central courtyard. Either the Littlefeathers had enjoyed more than one income or construction foremen were paid a hell of a lot more than Nash had imagined.

"Joy?" said a woman's voice on the intercom.

"No ma'am," he replied, putting his mouth close to the box. "My name's Nash Hansen, from the *Ledger*."

"What do you want?" The voice had changed from cheery to uncertain.

"I'd like to ask you a few questions about your husband," Nash said.

"What kind of questions?" She was edgy.

He knew if he didn't convince her quickly, she would stop talking and the security door would remain shut. "I think I know who killed him."

The buzzer sounded immediately.

★ ★ ★ ★ ★

"I was beginning to think nobody cared about what happened to Shane anymore," Tina Littlefeather said as she began folding towels on the laundry-room table.

She looked to be about forty-five and fighting, Nash thought. She had the pinched look of someone who had undergone more than one plastic surgery and her dark hair had been teased more than a fat kid in gym class. Her long fingernails kept snagging on the terry towels and she cursed several times under her breath.

"The police haven't called me in a month," she said after freeing her hand for the third time. "Last I heard there weren't even any suspects."

"I've got one for you," Nash said. He reached into the basket for a bath towel and began folding. "Did your husband ever say anything about a job Warren Construction was doing for Evan Carr?"

"Shane was finishing up those drive-in projects when he was killed," she said quietly. "Is there some connection?"

"Did Shane ever talk about the job?" he asked again.

"Nothing specific. He'd always tell me if there was a delay or if a member of his crew made a big mistake, that sort of thing."

"Who's Joy, Mrs. Littlefeather?" She was hiding something, and Nash knew he wasn't going to find out what it was by launching a frontal assault.

"What?"

"When I pressed the buzzer a few minutes ago, you thought I was someone named Joy."

"Oh," she said. "Joy's my housekeeper. You probably noticed I'm a little rusty on the domestic work." She gestured to the pile of badly folded linen.

Nash glanced down the hall into the living room. Several

changes of clothes lay crumpled on the floor and two pizza boxes were sprung open on the coffee table. "No offense, but it looks like you've been waiting for Joy for quite a while."

"I told her I could pay her as soon as the insurance check comes in," Tina Littlefeather said as she threw a half-folded towel back into the basket. "But they won't give me the settlement until the end of the investigation, and who knows when that will be. Joy's been good about it for the past few weeks, but she's got a family to support."

"Mrs. Littlefeather, was your husband engaged in some sort of fraud?" When he said it, she leaned against the table with both hands and took a deep breath.

"Off the record?" she asked. It seemed like every source liked to trot out that phrase. As he nodded, she began to wipe rivulets of tears off her cheeks with the backs of her hands. It looked like the dam was about to burst, so Nash placed a hand on Tina's right shoulder and guided her to a seat on the living-room couch.

After giving her a chance to blow her nose and take a drink of ice water, Nash continued the interview. With most of the tension drained from her face, she looked about five years younger.

"Shane had an agreement with some of Warren Construction's regular suppliers." She said it slowly, as if surprised to hear the words come out of her mouth. "They would bill the client for premium-grade insulation, say, even though they had installed a cheaper brand."

"And then Shane and the supplier would split the profits," Nash said.

She nodded. "He said all the crew chiefs did it."

It was coming easier now, he could see it in the way she leaned back into the deep cushions of the couch. For many people, Nash had found, talking to a journalist off the record was like sitting through confession without having to pay penance.

"At first I told him he ought to stop, that he was bound to get caught." She straightened up to look at him. "Do you know how many nasty looks a white woman gets around here when she marries a Native American?"

Nash shook his head.

"Even my friends made snide comments. They asked me if I chewed the leather on his boots at the end of the day to make them soft, or if he could be trusted not to steal their dogs for dinner. They'd say these stupid, hurtful things and then be surprised when I didn't laugh right along with them."

Tina took a gulp of water and looked as if she might begin crying again. Nash reached for the box of tissue, but she waved him off.

"Shane and I loved each other so much, but I still needed to show those people, to prove we were better than them. And when that extra cash started coming in, sometimes thousands of dollars a month . . . Well, after a very short time it was impossible to say no.

"Within six months, we had the nicest car on the block, a brand new Thunderbird, amusingly enough. Six months after that, we said goodbye to our cruddy duplex apartment and to our stupid friends. We had a nice condo, a maid. We had respect. But when Shane overheard Reese Stevens talk about using the drive-in to stockpile weapons, we got greedy."

Nash whistled softly. "Gunrunning?"

Tina nodded slowly. "On an early inspection of the Star-Time project, Reese thanked Spice Warren and Evan Carr for helping him carry out his 'patriotic duty to arm our friends to the south.' Shane threatened to expose Carr unless he gave us a fifty-thousand-dollar payoff. And then they killed him."

Tina's tears were coming faster now and she gratefully accepted a wad of tissue from Nash.

"I couldn't tell the police what had happened," she said between sobs. "They would have taken everything. Our condo, our reputation. Everything."

"I understand," Nash said, reaching over to pat her hand. He also understood that Tina knew she could end up in jail as an accomplice to fraud if the entire story came out. Unfortunately, like a priest, Nash was obliged by the ethics of his profession to keep all off-the-record confessions to himself. Unless, of course, he could get another source to corroborate the information independently, which was exactly what he intended to do.

And with illegal arms shipments added to the list of Evan Carr's transgressions, there wouldn't be enough Hail Marys in the world to save him now.

Watching TV in his room at the Colton Holiday Inn that evening, Nash couldn't help thinking about the Wendy and Bill situation. Maybe he had just come home to break up with her for good. The only way to know for sure was to talk to her, but he couldn't risk letting anyone else know he was in town.

Nash knew of only one other way to get a handle on the situation, and they would have to be out of the apartment for it to work. He felt like a slimeball as he dialed Wendy's number, but it was definitely time for desperate measures.

"Hi, this is Wendy McConnell," the message started, but Nash didn't have time to listen to the rest of it. He was busy punching three-digit sequences into the phone in hopes of finding her message retrieval code. He'd owned enough answering machines to know that most manufacturers did little to protect the privacy of their customers. The code would most likely be something simple, like 111, or 112, even 123.

Bingo. He heard a series of beeps and waited for the messages. There were two.

"Bill, where are you? I only left for work an hour ago." Wendy sounded playfully upset. "I'm going to try and get off early, so keep the covers warm, okay? Uh-oh, looks like a party of ten. Gotta go. Love you."

The second message was from Bill. He was calling from what sounded like a pretty rowdy country-western bar, especially for a Sunday night.

"I might be a little late tonight, honey," he yelled. "I'm partying with some buds down at the Lazy X. If you get home early, why don't you come on down?"

Nash hung up and flopped over on his stomach. The pillowcase was cool on his face, but it smelled of cigar smoke. He waited several minutes for the feeling of numbness to subside, then he opened the mini-bar and began lining the airline-sized bottles of booze on the counter, next to his waiting glass.

Chapter Twenty-two

Nash was ten minutes late calling Carl Barns at the gas-station pay phone. He had lost track of the time sitting in the steam-filled bathroom with his head in his hands, trying to clear the toxins out of his system.

"Don't you own a watch?" Carl asked.

"Don't start," Nash said as he lay crosswise on the bed. "I'm barely alive."

"I'd say the same thing about Curt Escobar, by the looks of it."

"You saw Curt?" Nash jerked into a sitting position so suddenly that he almost blacked out.

"Two guys dumped him into the trunk of a car yesterday afternoon," Carl said. There was a long pause. "I think he was alive."

"What do you mean you think?"

"Why didn't you tell me, Nash? Why didn't you call the police?"

"What do you mean you think?" Nash yelled.

"He was handcuffed, for one thing," Carl said. "I don't think they'd cuff a dead man. And I think I saw his leg moving before they closed the trunk."

"Okay. I'm sorry I got angry." Nash pressed his free hand hard against his forehead. Things are really getting out of control here, he thought.

"Why didn't you tell me?" Carl asked again. "Shit, Curt

and I have been friends since almost the first day he came to the *Ledger*."

When Nash told him about Snipes' threat and reminded him of Escobar's difficult relationship with the police, Carl calmed down somewhat.

"Did you by any chance follow the car?" Nash asked.

"You told me to stay on the roof."

"I'm just asking."

"No, I didn't follow the car," Carl said. "I couldn't tail a turd in the sewer. But I did do the job you asked me to do."

"What did you see?" Nash took a sip of lukewarm tap water.

"I got faces and plates like you said. I shot three rolls of the flock unloading a moving van full of weapons into the snack bar. Stevens and Snipes were directing the whole operation."

"What kind of weapons?"

"Grenades, mortars, rocket launchers, ammunition, you name it."

"You've got pictures of Stevens and Snipes in the act?"

"The works."

"How many people altogether?"

"About twenty-five. Not counting the children."

Nash thought of Janie and Sarah Miller lying open-mouthed in a Dumpster full of cabbage. He wondered how crazy and stupid a man would have to be to drag his family into a mess like that. "How many kids?"

"Half a dozen or so. They were over on the playground in front of the main screen until it was time to go inside for morning services."

"Make two prints of every good shot you have," Nash said. "One for the feds and one for the papers."

"That's going to take all day."

"The sooner we have those prints, the sooner we find Escobar."

"I'll get right on it."

Nash set up an appointment to call Carl at the gas station again Tuesday afternoon, then fell back into bed for an extra two hours of sleep.

He found several books about the history of North American trapping in the library of the University of California at Riverside. After two hours of research, Nash discovered the perfect historical figures to use in his plan to snare Evan Carr: the founders of the Hudson's Bay Company, Pierre Radisson and Medard Chouart des Groseilliers.

Although he had never seen any streets named after them in Chicago, Radisson and Groseilliers had been as instrumental in opening the continent to trade as LaSalle, Marquette, and Balboa were.

The Catholic Groseilliers hooked up with the Huguenot Radisson by marrying his sister Marguerite at the Three Rivers settlement near Quebec in 1656. From that moment, the two adventurers made a career of hatching wild schemes to create great Canadian fur monopolies that invariably led France and England to the brink of war in the region.

The more Nash read about the creation of one of history's great mercantile economies, the better he understood Evan Carr's fascination with the fur-trapping era. Here was a time, from the early seventeenth century to the middle eighteen hundreds, in which ultimate free-market capitalism was practiced. The trappers came in even before the merchants and the missionaries. The great Company became so ingrained in frontier society that the native tribes jokingly claimed its initials stood for "Here Before Christ."

Nash wondered if Evan Carr ever imagined himself commander of an early trading fort on Hudson's Bay, sitting next to a fire, holding a royal warrant from King Charles I and waiting for the Assiniboine and Cree to bring in a fresh pile of beaver pelts he could benevolently exchange for a few barrels of flour and sugar.

If so, Carr would certainly count Radisson and Groseilliers among his heroes, Nash concluded as he read an account of their lives:

Thought to have been the first Europeans to explore the Upper Mississippi, they arrived in the area of present-day Minnesota in 1659, a full fourteen years before the Jesuit Priest Marquette had set out with the trapper Joliet to find the "Father of Waters." The energetic brothers-in-law learned of an easy water route from the Atlantic to Hudson's Bay from a band of Huron they traded with along the way. It was information that would soon change their lives, and the face of the New World, forever.

Although most of Nash's classmates had hated the backgrounding segment of their news-writing class at Northwestern, he had always received top marks for his detailed story research. But this project was the real deal, he thought as he pored over the books. If he didn't have every base covered going into the sting he was planning for tomorrow, Carr might get away. He read on.

A few years after returning to Canada to set up an independent trapping operation, Radisson and Groseilliers became dissatisfied with the restrictions placed upon them by the Hundred Associates, a regional fur monopoly chartered by Louis XIV. But when the adventurers asked Jean Talon, Intendant of Quebec, for permission to set up shop on the virgin waters of the Bay in 1663, he asked for a fifty-percent kickback on any fur they brought back. After they balked at the deal, the Intendant banned them from going altogether.

Petty extortion and capricious use of power. Talon would have fit right in with the Chicago City Council, Nash thought.

Displaying remarkably poor judgment, Radisson and Groseilliers had set out for the Bay in direct violation of Talon's official decree. Although they hauled out some three hundred thousand dollars' worth of pelts after only one year, upon their return to Quebec the governor had them arrested and put Groseilliers in jail for a considerable stretch. When all the fines had been paid, they had only about twenty thousand left to show for their efforts.

By 1665, having wised up considerably, the intrepid partners decided to switch to the British side. After arriving in London, Radisson and Groseilliers excited Prince Rupert with tales of bountiful lands where organized competition was seemingly nonexistent. So successful was their pitch that they re-entered the half-million square miles of the Bay in 1670 as Rupert's main agents in the New World. Holding a charter from Charles I authorizing the formation of a Hudson's Bay Company, R&G had the power "to get out ships of war, to erect forts, make reprisals, send home all English subjects entering the Bay without license, and to declare war and make peace with any people not Christians."

What king had given Evan Carr *carte blanche* to erect his underground fort, make threats, run guns and murder with impunity? Nash wondered.

The establishment of Prince Rupert's empire was going smoothly until a band of Frenchmen showed up at the Company's four new Hudson's Bay forts. When this unexpected turn of events led the English to accuse Radisson and Groseilliers of treachery, the flexible French duo promptly deserted the HBC and realigned themselves with their countrymen.

Groseilliers eventually became so mistrusted by both sides

that he retired from the trade completely. But in later years, Radisson went through the revolving door one more time, bringing his prosperous fort back into the service of England and the mighty Company. And even though he retired with a small pension, the old bushranger was used to such high living that he left behind a mountain of debt for the HBC to clean up after he died.

Radisson had been loyal only to money and power throughout his life, and now he would be the key to bringing down the equally bankrupt Evan Carr, Nash thought. He couldn't have come up with a more ironic coda to the story if he'd tried.

After studying the types of beaver traps in common use during the seventeenth century, Nash began putting the final component of his plan into action. He took the Los Angeles and New York phone books from the research room and started tracking down Mr. Harvey, the auctioneer whose name he had read from one of Evan Carr's memos.

The fifth auction house he called from the lobby payphone informed him that Harvey was the owner of a large antiques store in nearby Westwood. He hung up and dialed the number. When Nash mentioned Carr's name to the receptionist, she patched him right through to the executive office.

"Blaine Harvey," said the voice on the other end of the line.

"Good afternoon, sir," Nash began. "My name is Xavier Plum and I am a curiosity dealer from Ottawa. I understand you have dealings with a noted collector of animal traps."

"Yes, Mr. Carr is a regular customer of mine." Harvey had a sophisticated, melancholy lilt to his voice that Nash found oddly pleasing.

But when Nash asked if he had ever heard of Pierre

Radisson, the antique dealer gasped like a schoolboy at his first peep show.

"The founder of the Hudson's Bay Company?" he asked.

"One and the same," Nash said. "I have here a fine trap of his with Mr. Carr's name written all over it." He allowed himself a tiny smile.

"Do tell," Harvey said.

"Radisson used the trap to catch beaver near Quebec in 1664," Nash continued. "I, ah, came into possession of it there recently."

The scribbling stopped. "Mr. Plum, this trap did not come from an institutional collection, I presume."

"I obtained the piece from a private estate sale," Nash said. "It comes complete with authentication papers from the historical society in Ottawa. I think you'll agree this trap could become the centerpiece of Mr. Carr's collection."

"Indeed," Harvey said thoughtfully. "I'm just wondering why you didn't approach Mr. Carr on your own."

"I'm only in the area for a few days and I wanted to set up a meeting quickly, through an intermediary Evan Carr could trust."

"Very prudent, Mr. Plum. What sort of arrangement did you have in mind?"

"There would be a respectable commission for you, of course," Nash said. "Say five percent?"

"Say ten."

"Agreed." He certainly was a greedy little shit. But ten percent of nothing was still nothing. "I'd like to set up a brief meeting with Mr. Carr for mid-morning tomorrow. Perhaps at his country club, if he belongs to one."

"He does."

"Would that arrangement be amenable?"

"I'll see what I can do."

Nash asked Harvey to leave word of the appointment at the Riverside Sheraton. Then he put in a call to Homer, the next Mr. Xavier Plum.

They met in the Riverside Mall. Homer, dressed in his full Berdoo Angels denims, was eating an Orange Julius hot dog and dripping mustard all over his fingers. He would need a complete make-over if they were going to pull off this stunt, Nash thought as he led Homer into a Supercuts.

"I'm never going to live this down," Homer said as a young stylist fastened a plastic bib around his neck.

"Just lean your head back into the sink," she said.

"I've been cultivating this look for seventeen years," he pleaded. "Hey, keep that shampoo out of my eyes."

The woman straightened up and put her hands on her hips. "Look, I'm not getting paid enough to take this crap," she said to Nash. "Does he want a cut or doesn't he?"

"He does, he does," Nash said as Homer shook his head no, sending a spray of water onto the stylist. Nash handed her a twenty. "For your trouble."

"What do I get for my trouble?" Homer whimpered.

"A kick in the teeth if you don't shut up," Nash said.

"You heard the man," the woman said as she twisted a towel tight on Homer's head. "Now, what type of cut did you have in mind?"

"What about a sort of late-period Dennis Hopper?" Nash asked. "The well-heeled rebel look."

"Yeah," Homer concurred, stroking his whiskers thoughtfully.

"And lose the beard," Nash said. Before Homer could object, he added, "Hey, we're trying to save lives here."

After twenty minutes of hell for everyone, the stylist

held up a mirror to Homer's head. With the collar-length cut and clean-shaven chin, even Homer had to admit he looked ten years younger. And just respectable enough, Nash thought.

By the time the mall closed, Homer's costume was ready to go. He wore a double-breasted jacket, Harris tweed slacks, a solid silk tie, and Italian loafers. A dark pair of Serengeti Drivers with tortoise-shell frames completed the look.

"You're the hippest Canadian since Alanis Morissette," Nash said admiringly.

"Gee, thanks," Homer replied, twisting around to see the cut of his slacks in the department store mirror. "I look like a fucking game-show host."

Back at the hotel, Nash picked up a message from Blaine Harvey: The meeting was set for eight-thirty the next morning at the Arrowhead Country Club.

Over a pitcher of beer at the Sheraton bar, Nash drilled Homer on the history of trapping and the rudiments of their plan.

"So I'm supposed to be from Quebec?" Homer asked. He pronounced it K-Beck.

"No," Nash said. "You're Xavier Plum from Ottawa, but you picked up the trap from a private collection in Quebec." While Homer repeated his cover story, Nash ordered another pitcher.

"What should I do if he invites me to stay for breakfast?" Homer asked.

"Go ahead and order something. But when the waiter leaves, bring Carr out to the Olds to show him the trap."

"Gotcha." Homer refilled the pilsner glasses with the skill of a bartender in a beer commercial.

"Remember, you have to park in a fairly secluded spot,"

Nash continued. "And don't keep me waiting out there too long."

Homer nodded. "I've been thinking."

"About what?"

"Kidnapping, murder, right-wing kooks." Homer paused and raised his glass. "You know, it just doesn't get any better than this."

Chapter Twenty-three

A few minutes before Xavier Plum's appointment with Carr, Homer pulled the Olds behind a gas station near the country club and Nash climbed into the trunk. They had stowed the spare tire in the hotel room (much to the displeasure of their maid), but still Nash found his heels almost touching the backs of his thighs as he crammed his five-foot, ten-inch frame as far into the wheel well as he could reasonably manage.

"It's only three blocks," Homer said as he eased down the trunk lid.

"I'd better not smell pancakes on your breath when you come out with Carr," Nash said as the crack of light disappeared into a deep, black void.

"What was that?" Homer asked, chuckling. "Couldn't quite make out that last part."

The shocks and suspension on the Olds provided a relatively smooth ride. As the car cruised into the country club parking lot, Nash wondered how bumpy Escobar's trip had been, or if he'd even been awake to notice.

Nash couldn't see the dial of his watch, but judging by the fact that the short drive had seemed to last at least twenty minutes, he settled in for a long wait. Although it was not yet mid-morning, the cramped quarters had warmed up quickly, and he pulled his T-shirt up over his nose to filter out the oppressive smell of hot plastic.

As rivulets of sweat began to trickle down his neck and the backs of his legs, Nash remembered the last time he'd been forced to face his claustrophobia. Early that summer he had gone to a street carnival on the North Side of Chicago where the rides were so caked with grease that the drippings gave the grass a brown patina. His date had been leery of the big attraction—a three-car train that did a loop-the-loop while the track itself turned end over end—but he had teased her into giving it a try. The ride had made him feel like he was in the middle of a giant gyroscope, a pleasant enough sensation. But when the train stopped, the attendant had looked in on them with a puzzled expression instead of opening up the bubble top and setting them free.

"I can't get it open," the young carny had yelled to his partner as he pried on the edge of the dome. Suddenly, Nash felt himself straining hard against the shoulder harness pinning him against the molded plastic seat. He imagined having to wait for the fire department to come and cut them out of the car with an acetylene torch. When Nash looked to his date for reassurance, she had turned away as if to punish him. He began humming under his breath to keep himself from screaming.

"Would you please stop?" She had said it without even bothering to look at him.

Three minutes later, when the carny finally realized that the train was simply facing the wrong way, Nash found he had bitten his lower lip until it started to bleed. As soon as the train returned to its normal position, his date had climbed out of the car almost casually. As he stood next to the Whack-a-Mole game with his hands braced on his knees to keep from hyperventilating, Nash had watched her step into a taxi and drive straight out of his life.

A particularly ticklish bead of sweat wending its way down

his right calf brought Nash back to attention. Placing the Redhawk carefully next to his head, he pulled his lower legs tight against his thighs and started to rub away the itch.

Feeling a familiar twinge behind both knees, Nash stopped scratching and let go of the shins, but it was too late. As the calf muscles in both legs spasmed and twisted into tight, baseball-sized knots, he began to flail about in an attempt to ease the excruciating pain. Forcing himself to breathe deeply, Nash stopped flopping around the trunk and began flexing his feet instead, allowing his legs to slowly uncramp.

He was finally beginning to feel some of the tension drain out of his body when he heard voices approaching the car. In a panic, Nash groped for the now-misplaced revolver, causing his leg spasms to return with a vengeance.

When Homer released the trunk lid, Evan Carr yelped in surprise as Nash jolted into a sitting position and began furiously kneading out the cramps.

"Where's the gun?" Homer asked.

"Grab him," Nash yelled, but by then Carr was already in motion.

Lunging forward, he slammed the trunk lid down onto Nash's head and turned to run.

As blood began streaming down Nash's face from a gash on his forehead, he looked up to see a clump of slick, matted hair hanging from the trunk latch and then fainted dead away.

Chapter Twenty-four

When he awoke, Nash found he was still in the trunk of the Olds. He didn't know quite what had happened or how long he had been out. Unconscious, his body had relaxed enough to ease the cramps in his legs, but his face was sticky with blood and his head was pounding like a heavy surf.

As the car slowed to a halt, Nash reached behind his head and felt around for a tire iron, anything heavy. Instead, he found the Redhawk lying next to his left ear. He couldn't believe Carr would be stupid enough to leave the gun with him in the trunk, but there it was. And this time, he thought as the key turned in the lock, things were going to turn out a little bit differently.

"Freeze, asshole!" Nash yelled as he pointed the .44 at Homer's face.

"Whoa! It's me, amigo. It's me," Homer repeated, raising his hands.

"Sorry," Nash said. "I thought you were Carr."

"First he nearly kills me, then he insults me." Homer gave Nash a hand out of the trunk. "Why don't you stretch your legs a minute and I'll fill you in."

They were in a heavily wooded area of the foothills. Looking around, Nash was surprised to see shell casings all over the deserted gravel parking lot.

"We're at the Lytle Creek target range," Homer explained. "But there's no shooting today. Fire danger's too high."

"What the hell is going on?" Nash asked.

"After you cramped up and ruined our ambush, Carr smacked you in the melon with the trunk lid." Homer leaned over to inspect the cut on Nash's head. "Looks like it's a pretty bad one, too."

"That much I know."

"At least it's stopped bleeding." Homer was sounding more concerned by the minute. "Are you feeling woozy or anything? I hope you don't have a concussion."

"I'm fine. Now would you please tell me why you left me in the trunk all the way to Lytle Creek?"

"After Carr hit you, he shouted for help before I could cold-cock him. Some people started running toward us from across the parking lot, so I just closed the lid on you, tossed Carr in the backseat and hit the gas. I didn't exactly have time for the social niceties."

"Thanks for saving my ass." Nash was starting to feel dizzy, like he was going to black out again. He sat on the lip of the trunk and tried to make his eyes focus.

"I think it's time to get you some help," Homer said.

"In a minute." He didn't feel quite so bad now that he was sitting down. "We're not going anywhere until I ask Evan Carr a few questions."

Homer dragged Carr from the floor of the Olds feet-first and dropped him unceremoniously onto the gravel.

"He's pretty tough for an old guy," Homer said. "I stopped at an abandoned gas station to put this duct tape on him, and damned if he didn't wake up and try to fight me again. And you know how much I hate to be obstructed."

Homer punctuated this last statement by giving Carr a sharp kick in the side, then helped him into a sitting position against the car.

"My friend here would like to have a few words with you."

Homer pointed toward Nash with his sunglasses. "How does that sound?"

Carr shouted something unintelligible into the duct tape.

"What?" Homer asked. "Oh, that's right." He grasped a corner of the tape. "You can't answer any questions until I pull this off."

With that, Homer yanked hard and Carr cursed as the gag tore loose.

"That's going to be some tender meat for a couple days, pard," Homer said as Carr licked his lips.

"Afternoon, Mr. Carr." Nash raised the gun with both hands and aimed it at Evan Carr's chest. "I need some fast answers."

"I'll stomp you like a grape," Carr replied, sitting up as straight as he could manage with his hands taped behind his back.

"That's not what I wanted to hear," Nash said. He cocked the revolver with his right thumb and held it steady.

"You're a two-bit punk and you have no idea the trouble you've gotten yourself into," Carr said evenly. "Have you ever heard of a drowning set?"

"Can't say as I have."

"That's when you lay a string of traps along the normal water route of an animal, like a beaver. That way, when the beaver gets caught in one of them, there's no chance he'll try to gnaw his leg off and escape. If he does, you see, he'll drown.

"You always have to be smarter than your prey, Mr. Hansen, because the survival instinct is very strong. So unless you're quite prepared to kill me right here, right now, you might as well let me go, because I'm not going to tell you anything."

"He's smooth, I'll give him that," Nash said.

"Shoot him," Homer said.

"But I need some answers first."

"I'm sure Reese Stevens or Spice Warren know at least as much as he does," Homer said. "Besides, you've already established that you left the city, what, two days ago?"

"That's true."

"You're both full of shit," Carr said. He spat in Nash's direction. "Go ahead and shoot, for all the good it'll do you."

That does it, Nash thought. He picked out a kneecap. "Where's Escobar? Under one of your drive-ins?"

"I don't know what you're talking about," Carr replied.

"The reporter you had kidnapped. Where is he?"

"Doesn't ring any bells."

Nash pulled the trigger and the Redhawk reared back ferociously in his hand. The noise made his head throb. He would need to sit down again soon.

"Ding dong," Homer said as Carr inched away from the place where the bullet had splatted into the gravel.

"I think we can come to some agreement here," Carr said. His voice was still smooth, but his arms had begun to shake.

"Now, about Escobar," Nash said.

"I'm not lying about that." Carr glanced uneasily at the gun. "Reese Stevens and I are, ah, unwilling business partners."

"Do tell," Nash said, cocking the revolver again and resting it on his cast.

"We were partners in a used-car lot back in the fifties. We met in Korea and became friends after we found out we were from the same area. But that friendship ended in 1958."

"And why was that?"

"I discovered irregularities in the books which Reese could not adequately explain. We sold the dealership and parted ways shortly thereafter, and that's the last I saw of him until three years ago, when he launched his bid for the mayor's seat. He came to me looking for a campaign favor."

"He had the gall to ask you for a contribution?" Nash asked.

"My thoughts exactly," Carr replied. "I asked him to leave my office at once, but then he laid out a deal that seemed too good to be true. Which, of course, it was. But I must admit I fell for it. Reese said he had been approached by a group of extremists calling themselves the Four Oaks. They were involved in drugs, guns, extortion, you name it—all to raise money for a series of paramilitary survivalist camps. To give you an idea of how crazy they are, the Four Oaks are God, law, loyalty, and family."

"What about truth?" Nash asked.

"Who needs truth when you've got God and the law on your side?"

"Sounds like kind of a post-apocalyptic Boy Scouts."

"Exactly," Carr said. "But they were rich Boy Scouts looking for political clout. They agreed to fund Reese's campaign if he would provide a respectable front for their operations in Southern California. It was their idea to dig bunkers under the drive-ins. But they wanted to build them without any official scrutiny."

"And that's where you come in, as a respectable pillar of the community," Nash said.

"Yes." Carr pushed at the gravel with his heels to keep himself from sliding further down the car door.

"How'd you pull it off so easily?"

"It was hardly easy," Carr said. "We only completed the infrastructure at the Star-Time. That neighborhood's pretty desolate, as you've seen, and the wrap-around fence keeps out anyone who might straggle by. The other two theaters are in much more crowded areas. Besides, there's a good chance the city will be building a new convention center near the

Star-Time in the next few years, so that looks to be the most lucrative site by far, potentially."

"What's a new business district without a few office buildings?" Nash asked.

"Exactly," Carr continued. "We sealed off the theater for renovations, brought in the excavating equipment at night, then built a garage and supports for a ten-story tower. At double the normal rate, Warren's crews jumped at the chance to work evening overtime. Of course, we'll have to lay in the car ramps later. For now, the garage is accessible through a stairway entrance under the snack bar."

"Sounds like a lot of trouble to go to for one project," Nash said.

Carr smiled. "Reese said that if I would act as a figurehead, the organization would pay to purchase and remodel all three theaters, but the deeds would remain in my name. I'd get a cut of the legitimate profits from the drive-ins as well as a monthly tribute of ten thousand dollars from Snipes for as long as the Four Oaks used the properties. Then, when they left, I'd have three prime sites for offices or apartments, at absolutely no cost."

Homer whistled. "Where can I get in on a set-up like that?"

"Trust me, you wouldn't want to," Carr said. "I figured Reese had no chance of winning the race, and I was right. And with no protection, I thought the Four Oaks would stick around for perhaps six months before the local and federal authorities started closing in on him. Then I'd blame my 'manager,' Snipes, for starting a cult and I'd admit to having violated zoning laws. I'd say I didn't get a permit for the parking garage because I didn't want to upset the drive-in preservationists, and that I knew once I'd excavated the site, protesters wouldn't be able to shut down my construction plans.

"But it hasn't worked out that way," Carr continued. "As soon as Reese lost the election, he and Spice Warren got heavily involved in setting up some kind of Latin American arms deal with Snipes. It was a natural for them; they were involved in every two-bit patriotic enterprise that came down the pike, including Iran-Contra.

"After a few months, the money from Snipes dried up and it looked like things were getting pretty far out of hand. I thought about going to the authorities, but if I knew about the deal, obviously I was implicated right along with Reese and Warren. I had to take matters into my own hands."

"The trap?" Nash asked.

"The trap," Carr agreed. "I needed to send Snipes a message without going to the authorities. I figured if I had to wait for the properties, I should at least get the ten thousand a month."

"Kind of a Mexican stand-off," Nash said. "You couldn't expose them for fear of going to jail and they needed you to keep the law out of their hair."

Carr nodded. "I've kept Snipes under surveillance. The shipment is due to leave soon, probably this week. After that, I plan to wash my hands of the whole affair and expose their little cult."

"As soon as it's no longer dangerous for you," Nash said. "As soon as the weapons are safely, untraceably out of the country. Without the rocket launchers and grenades, the Four Oaks becomes nothing more than an embarrassment."

"And what's wrong with that?"

"After he completes the shipment, Snipes can escape with his profits while Warren and Reese Stevens probably get off with a slap on the wrist."

"A pity," Carr said.

"And who answers for the deaths of the Miller family?" Nash asked.

"Who?"

"Members of the church Snipes had killed."

"I don't know anything about that."

"But you do know about Shane Littlefeather."

"He was Warren's foreman on the drive-in projects," Carr replied. "He got greedy and he got killed. The way I understand it, Reese found out Littlefeather was cheating him on the materials and someone, probably Snipes, made him pay."

"The way I understand it, when Littlefeather threatened to expose you, you ordered a hit on him." Nash steadied the Redhawk. "I heard you were in on this arms deal from the beginning."

"You're mistaken."

"So you've simply been an unfortunate victim of circumstance here, is that it?"

"I thought I could get something for nothing. As usual, that was a mistake. But I never set out to harm anyone."

"No, you only set a trap that almost cut off a man's foot, killed another man to protect your position, and stood by while a gang of thugs murdered a family, kidnapped a journalist, and stockpiled enough weapons to pull off a *coup d'etat* every week till Christmas. You smell like a real fucking rose here."

"Mr. Hansen, if you're quite finished, might I suggest that we would both stand to benefit from some medical attention?"

"He's right, Nash," Homer said. "He's told us everything we need to know."

"Not quite," Nash said. "When are you supposed to pick up your next payment from Snipes?"

"Tomorrow afternoon. We're to meet at the Star-Time at three."

"I want you to call and reschedule for later today."

"Impossible."

"It's either that or lose your knees." Nash steadied the .44 and cocked it again.

"I'll see to it."

"That's better. And when you call, tell Snipes that if he kills Escobar, he can kiss his arms shipment goodbye. Tell him you need to see him alive or all bets are off."

Chapter Twenty-five

After untaping Carr's hands and watching him make a cell-phone call to Malcolm Snipes, Homer drove Nash and Carr to the Loma Linda Medical Center, a university hospital just west of San Bernardino.

"If you play straight with me this afternoon at the Star-Time, I'll tell the authorities you helped to free Escobar and set up a sting on Snipes and Stevens of your own free will," Nash said as he cut the duct tape off Carr's wrists in the hospital parking lot.

"Agreed." Carr began rubbing the white, sticky tape backing off of his wrists. "I shall be waiting for the forces of justice at four this afternoon."

Nash looked at his watch. It was almost eleven-forty-five.

Carr said, "I'll be glad to wash my hands of this whole affair and get on with my life."

Fat chance, Nash thought as they made their way inside.

Within five minutes, an orderly had stopped by the registration desk to deliver Carr to the X-ray room. By noon, Nash found himself sitting on the edge of an examination table in a curtained-off section of the emergency room.

"Why'd you make a deal like that with Carr?" Homer asked as they waited for the doctor.

"Even if Carr avoids being implicated in the arms deal, there's no way he's going to skate on income-tax charges,"

Nash said. "Think about it, he never paid a cent for any of the drive-ins or the remodeling, yet they're in his name. And you can bet he never reported the monthly kick-back from Snipes on his 1040."

"What about Shane Littlefeather?"

"After we bring down the Four Oaks and get Escobar back, we'll give all the information we have to the district attorney. Maybe they'll be able to make a case against Evan Carr."

"But you doubt it."

"I think the best shot at putting Carr behind bars is the tax angle. Just like with Al Capone, it's the only area where he couldn't cover his tracks."

"So he does a stretch at the Club Fed in Boron, so what?"

"So his reputation is ruined, his freedom is taken away for a few years, at the very least. And remember, we're also stopping the arms shipment and bringing down Snipes and Stevens in the process. We might even be able to implicate Spice Warren."

"I still think you should have shot him while you had the chance," Homer said as the doctor pulled back the curtain.

"Nash Hansen?" he asked, flipping through the admission forms. "Let's take a look at that head."

After fifteen minutes of poking, prodding, and inspecting of pupils, the resident told Nash he had suffered a minor concussion.

"I want you to go straight to bed," he said as he cleansed and stitched the gash on Nash's head. "And if there's an onset of dizziness or blurry vision, I want your friend to drive you right back here so we can put you under observation."

Homer nodded as the doctor explained what to look for in the way of pupil dilation, odd behavior and other possible adverse side effects from the blow.

158

★ ★ ★ ★ ★

Homer drove them back to the apartment. There was no need to maintain the pretense they had left town now that Carr had seen them. Nash doubted Snipes would be keeping an eye on the building now that the shipment was ready to go, and he knew Homer was itching to get back into his regular clothes.

As they merged onto the I-10, Nash caught Homer glancing over to examine his eyes.

"Quit staring at me," Nash said.

"Doctor's orders," Homer replied.

"Give me those." Nash pulled the Serengeti Drivers from Homer's nose.

"That's not fair. I paid for those," he said as Nash donned the sunglasses.

"The doctor said I needed to rest my eyes. You wouldn't want me to start getting dizzy and passing out onto your lap, would you?"

"Okay, but I want the glasses back as soon as you're better," Homer said. "Little thief," he added under his breath.

While Homer took a shower and changed back into his denims, Nash called Carl Barns for an update. "What's the scoop?"

"Still no sign of Escobar," Carl said. "The newsroom's really starting to worry. He's missed two shifts now, and Lydia called in a missing person's to the police."

"You haven't said anything, have you?"

"Not yet, but I'm starting to wonder why. The cops don't seem too interested in looking for Curt, and now we're planning to run a story on his disappearance in tomorrow's editions."

"Would it make you feel better to know that Snipes is bringing Escobar back to the drive-in in two hours?" Nash asked.

"You're kidding. Have you called in the feds?"

Nash told the photographer about his deal with Carr. "I'm not calling anybody until I see Escobar with my own eyes," Nash said. "I don't trust Carr not to pull something."

"What can I do?" Carl asked.

"Get back up on that roof with your fancy camera and start shooting when the meeting begins. If Escobar's there, we'll call in the cops and wrap this whole thing up."

"What if they don't bring him?"

"I'm still working on that one," Nash said.

At three, a knock on the door brought Nash out of a light sleep. As he sat up on the couch, he saw Homer grab the Redhawk from the coffee table and gesture at him to get down.

"Who is it?" Homer asked, standing beside the door with the .44 raised in front of his face.

"It's Wendy, your neighbor from down the hall."

Nash raised his head and nodded. Homer tucked the gun in his waistband, letting his shirttail fall over it, and opened the door.

"Nash?" she said as he stood up. "I thought you were gone." She was holding the pillow he had left on her bed the last night he'd spent with her.

"I've been looking all over for that," Nash said. "Come on in."

"I'm going to go check on my bike," Homer said as Wendy sat down at the kitchen table. "Be back in five minutes."

"Thanks," Nash said, picturing Homer's new Harley where he'd left it in the Sheraton parking lot.

"Nash, what happened to your head?" Wendy reached out to gently brush away the hair that had fallen over the white bandage. "And why are you here? What's going on?"

"I'm working undercover on the investigation I told you about at the Dodgers game. I would have let you know, but you seemed pretty busy at the time."

"I'm so glad you're here," she said, leaning over to give him a hug.

He didn't respond.

"I thought I'd never get a chance to explain everything to you," Wendy continued. "I thought you'd go through life hating me forever."

"Where's Bill?" Nash asked, trying to maintain a detached monotone.

"He's out looking for a job." She reached out and held Nash's hands in her slender fingers. "I know I've hurt you. And I'm sorry about the way this has turned out."

"Why should you be sorry?" he asked. "You had your little fling and now you've got your G.I. Joe. What more could you want?"

He thought she was going to slap him, but she started to cry instead.

"It's not like that at all." She wiped away the tears with the back of her left hand. "You and I shared some special time together. We both thought that time would last longer than it did."

"We did?" He feigned surprise.

"Quit beating up on me and listen for a minute." The fire had returned to her voice. "When you and I got together, I was finally giving up on Bill." She had stopped crying, but her cheeks were still streaked and shiny. "Like I said, he was career Army and there didn't seem to be any future in that for me. I always loved him, but I never thought he would give up the service. I'd resigned myself to that fact when he showed up on my doorstep holding a set of discharge papers."

"How'd that happen?"

"I guess Bill was as lonely for me in the Philippines as I was for him here. Nash, even when you and I were together, as good as it was, I still found myself thinking about him more than I should have. I guess I kept hoping he'd make some grand gesture to win me back."

"And he did," Nash said, so quietly he almost believed he was thinking it. But Wendy nodded. She'd heard him.

"When your biggest wish comes true, it isn't easy to turn your back on it," she said.

"Did he propose to you?"

"Not yet." A frown erased the dimple from her cheek. "But I'm hopeful. Once he settles back into civilian life, once we live together for a while, who knows?"

Nash had the urge to tell her that Bill wouldn't be able to find a job on the outside, that he'd miss his buddies in the service, that he'd re-up inside of six months and box Wendy into going with him. He wanted to say that in ten years she'd be looking at her third kid and her fifth base and her millionth TV dinner. But watching her soft, innocent smile return as she reached out to touch his cheek, he didn't say a word.

Instead, he took her hand, leaned forward and gave her a long, passionate kiss. He figured she owed him that much, and from the flushed look on her face as she got up to leave, he sensed she didn't mind too much. He'd let her go with fond memories, but he wanted at least a few of them to be bittersweet.

"Maybe I'll see you in the hall before you leave again," she said as she opened the door.

Nash nodded. He heard himself saying, "Take care of yourself."

And then she was gone.

He looked at his watch: Three-forty-five. Time to see a man about a kidnapped journalist.

Downstairs, Nash found Homer sitting in the Olds, blowing smoke rings out the window.

"You don't look so good," Homer said as Nash climbed behind the wheel.

"I'm not."

"I had a wife once," Homer said as they made their way to the Star-Time.

"What happened to her?"

"She decided I was aimless, that I'd never reach the potential she thought I had in high school."

"How old were you?"

"Eighteen when we got married, twenty-two when we split. She was a year younger, twenty-one going on forty."

"Was it messy?"

"Shit yes," Homer said, laughing. "The last year, Chloe started screwing around with my younger brother, Rich. He didn't know any better—he was only eighteen at the time. But Chloe, she thought, well, she might've been wrong about me ever being a success at anything, but that didn't mean my whole family was worthless."

"What happened?"

"The whole affair was happening under my nose, right under my roof even, for maybe three months. I didn't know what to do, Rich being my baby brother and all. And my parents, they didn't know a thing about it. I would've just as soon kept it that way, too, if I could only figure out how." Homer lit another cigarette, his third of the short trip.

"Anyway, one Friday night I get off shift early at the recycling center and I go to one of the neighborhood bars for a shot and a beer. And who should I see dancing Chloe around the barroom with his hand up her shirt right in front of about fifteen guys?"

"Rich?"

"You got it." Homer smacked the dashboard with his open palm. "Fucking Richie, feeling up my wife in front of the whole neighborhood."

"What'd you do?"

"What could I do? I beat the living shit out of both of them. Slapped Chloe around so hard her left eye swelled shut. Cracked Rich's skull with a pool cue. The whole works. So then the cops come, and Chloe and Rich press charges. I end up serving six months in the county slam, in which time Chloe divorces me and runs off with that little punk." He paused to take a long drag on the cigarette, letting the smoke cascade out of his nose, before continuing.

"Funny thing is, they have a couple of kids, Rich goes to college, gets a cushy job in a bank and they end up living happily ever after. And my parents, they never forgave me for beating them up. Never talked to me again."

"Was that supposed to cheer me up?"

"Hell no. I just wanted you to stop feeling so goddamn sorry for yourself. Put things in perspective. You met a cute girl, got laid a few times, and now you're clear of the whole deal. What's so bad about that, I ask you?"

"You sure do have a way with words, Homer."

"It's a gift, I will admit."

As they rounded the curved driveway into the Star-Time, Nash spotted three figures in front of the snack bar. "I think that's Escobar with Snipes and Carr," he said, pointing out the group.

"They're waiting for us," Homer said.

It looked as if Snipes was carrying an assault rifle, but Nash couldn't tell for sure if Carr was armed because his right hand was hidden behind Escobar's back.

"I say we call in the cops," Homer said.

"No. They've seen us. If we back out now, Curt's dead for sure."

"This looks too much like a set-up. I'm telling you, we should leave this one for the Mounties."

"If you want out, that's your choice," Nash said. "But if you're going, the time to get out is now."

"Count me in."

"Okay," Nash said as Homer pulled out the .44. "Let's talk strategy. If this is an ambush, and I'm inclined to agree with you on that score, would it be better for us to split up or stick together?"

"The best course of action when you're being set up is to do whatever it is they least expect you to do."

"I hope this thing has an airbag," Nash said as he backed the Olds just out of sight of the concession stand. "Ready?"

Homer rolled down his window and pulled the hammer back on the Magnum. "Hit it."

Nash pounded the accelerator and launched the Olds back around the corner and through the metal barricade hanging between the theater's two ticket booths. The car briefly caught air at the top of a speed bump and then skidded to a halt twenty yards from the concession stand as Homer opened the door and rolled out onto the gravel.

"Drop it," he said to Snipes, who was yanking back the cocking lever on his assault rifle.

As the weapon fell to the ground, Nash slowly got out of the car. "Afternoon, Curt," he said. "How's tricks?"

"I'm starting to lose that weight I've been worried about,"

Escobar said. "These folks have been fresh out of Twinkies ever since I got here."

"Go ahead and uncuff him," Homer said, tossing Nash the key chain he had retrieved from Snipes' belt.

"Not so fast," said Officer Klete Patterson, emerging from the snack bar with his service automatic drawn. Patterson unsheathed his nightstick with his free hand and gestured for Homer to drop the .44. He then sent Escobar sprawling face-first into the gravel with a vicious kick to the crook of his left knee. When Homer lunged to stop Escobar's fall, the officer swung the stick hard into Homer's solar plexus, doubling him over.

"You three are under arrest," Patterson said. He had an animal glint in his eye that spoke of several hits of high-grade crystal meth and a desire to kill. He turned to Escobar. "When Mr. Carr told me about the exchange, I knew your friends had to be working some type of double-cross, so I got here a bit early. Guess you're just going to have to start paying for your own lunches now." After delivering another vicious blow to Escobar's shoulders, Patterson turned to his other prisoners.

Nash anticipated his death more calmly than he ever would have thought possible. Regarding the twitching baton as an almost benign instrument, he closed his eyes and gave himself over to fate.

"That's enough," Evan Carr snapped. "We don't want any brutality charges at their trial."

Chapter Twenty-six

Sitting between Homer and Escobar in the squad car, Nash scooted as far forward on the seat as was comfortable. He hoped the voice-activated tape recorder he'd tucked into the front of his pants before they'd entered the drive-in would pick up a few more incriminating statements from Klete Patterson. If the wild-eyed officer was as high as he appeared to be, it wouldn't be too difficult to tape his exploits. The fact that Patterson's cursory pat-down had missed the recorder entirely gave Nash a bit of hope.

Because the cast on Nash's left wrist was too big to cuff, Patterson had shackled his right hand to a steel bar mounted on the back of the front seat. Escobar, still bleeding from his gravel facial, and Homer were cuffed behind their backs. Nash stretched his free hand across his body and began carefully brushing off the constellation of pebbles embedded in Escobar's chin.

"Keep that hand down or I'll beat it off with my baton," Patterson said as he watched Nash in the rearview.

"It's okay," Escobar whispered.

Nash noticed for the first time that blood was pooling up under the lens of Escobar's right eye. "My friend needs medical attention," Nash said.

"He's lucky he doesn't need a coroner," Patterson said.

"It's okay, Rambler," Escobar repeated. He was obviously having trouble breathing.

167

Nash hoped it wasn't broken ribs or a bruised lung. But since he wasn't getting anywhere with Patterson on the issue, he decided to take Escobar's advice and leave it alone. "How come you're riding solo today, Klete?"

"I'm on my lunch."

"Then your watch must be broken."

"I'm taking an early supper."

"Somebody should wipe that ugly smirk off your face," Homer said, throwing his knee hard into the back of the seat.

"You know, they told me I could kill you if I had to," Patterson said as he stopped for a red light. He unholstered his automatic and brought the barrel within an inch of Homer's nose.

"Who told you?" Nash asked. Homer glanced at him as if to say, *Who the hell cares?*

"They said you could all be jailhouse suicides after tomorrow, as far as they're concerned," Patterson continued. He was grinning. "You'd be surprised what a despondent inmate will use to off himself—shoelaces, clothes, ripped-up mattress covers. When they use the shoelaces, it generally takes them longer to die. I'm going to make sure the guards let you keep your shoelaces."

"Light's green," Escobar said. He stared straight into Patterson's eyes without blinking.

"What's tomorrow?" Nash asked as they got underway again.

"Wednesday," Patterson said.

"These guys who said you could kill us, are they some kind of religious kooks? No killing on Tuesdays?"

"I don't know and I don't give a flying fuck, smartass," the officer said. "All I know is, after tomorrow you stupid pricks are all mine."

"How much is Carr paying you for this?"

"None of your fucking business."

"But it is Carr who's paying you."

"No, it's the fucking Tooth Fairy." Patterson laughed loudly at his joke. "They may be paying me to keep you and your biker pal out of the way, but Escobar, him I'm doing strictly for pleasure."

"How'd Evan Carr know you had such a hard-on for Curt?" Nash asked. "Or did you approach him first? I bet you called him right after we asked for his file last week." He noticed that Patterson's expression had gone sullen. "He drew it all out of you, didn't he? With that mellow real-estate salesman voice of his, he had you spilling out years of hatred in five minutes. That's why you refused to help Escobar the last time he called you. And when the shit hits today, Carr gives you a buzz, tells you he's so grateful for the tip last week he'd like to throw a little bit of work your way. It's a dream come true: You get back at Curt, and you get paid to boot."

"You think you know so much." It was all Patterson could muster.

Nash could tell Klete was starting to lose the drug-induced edge, and he knew he had to push him hard before he came down too far. "They're sending out a big arms shipment tomorrow. Bet you didn't know that."

"Who gives a fuck?"

"Whoa, you didn't let me finish there, Einstein. The way I figure it, you're pulling an awful lot of exposure here for what, maybe ten thousand?"

From the surprised look in Patterson's eyes, Nash knew he'd hit it just about right.

"All I'm saying is, Carr and Snipes are going to pull down close to half a million bucks when those guns hit the border. I think you're getting the short end here, my friend."

"Carr's a good businessman, I respect him," Patterson said. Doubt was creeping into his voice. "He wouldn't cheat me."

Bingo. Nash hoped to Christ the tape hadn't run out yet.

"You're probably right," he said.

"Look," Patterson said, "you don't know what the hell you're talking about. I got a cush deal here. I arrest you for trespassing, assault, attempted murder, carrying an unlicensed firearm, and anything else I can think of, just so long as you stay put away until day after tomorrow. What I do after that is at my own discretion. For my troubles, I pull down ten large. So tell me, what's my beef here?"

"You're right," Nash said. "I'm sorry. I was way off-base thinking Carr would cheat you."

"Fucking-A." The officer nodded sagely.

As Patterson pulled the cruiser into the police parking lot, Nash let his hand wander under his shirttail. While the cop checked in with the lot attendant, Nash eased the tape out of the recorder and palmed it.

He saw his opportunity when Patterson stopped at the main desk to sign in before taking them in for searches and cell assignments. Nash held the confession tape under the lip of the scarred wooden counter and pressed it hard into an old wad of gum before Patterson turned to lead them away.

Patterson watched almost dreamily, coming down softly off his high, as another officer completed a full cavity search of Escobar and Homer in an exam room far off the station's beaten path. When Nash unzipped his pants, the tape recorder clattered to the floor.

"What the hell?" Patterson said, bending over to grab it. As he did, Homer stepped forward and kicked him in the face with his bare right foot, launching him into a wastebasket full of used rubber gloves. While Patterson was coming up with his nose bleeding and his gun drawn, the other officer grabbed a Taser off his desk and hit Homer with a jolt that sent him quivering to the floor.

"Who wants the next one?" Patterson asked, yanking out his baton. "Are you going to cooperate, or is this going to get ugly?"

"It already looks pretty ugly to me, Klete," Nash said, pointing to the two petroleum-jelly smeared gloves hanging luridly off the back of Patterson's pants.

"Dammit to hell." Patterson reached around with the nightstick to pry the gloves loose.

"You need me to call in some backup here?" the other officer asked, grinning.

"Shut up, Jeff."

"Bet it never gets this messy down in records," Jeff said.

"I'm warning you, man," Patterson said as he stood over the can trying to shake the gloves off his baton. Finally, he gave up and dropped the stick into the trash.

"What the hell are you doing bringing in perps, anyway?" Jeff asked as Homer came to and began to pull on his pants. His hands were still shaking and he looked like he didn't quite know where he was.

"I borrowed a squad to go get a burrito," Patterson said. "I saw a disturbance at the Star-Time on my way by."

"That's a long drive for a burrito."

"Who fucking asked you? Are you going to help me finish searching these guys or not?"

"Sorry, Klete."

"Just shut up, all right?" Patterson turned to face Nash again. "What the hell is this supposed to be?" He pointed to the tape recorder, which was still sitting where it had fallen.

"I use it to pick up women. They can't resist a talking crotch."

Patterson picked up the recorder and thrust it into Nash's face. "I'll make you eat this."

"You wouldn't happen to have any hot sauce left over from your burrito, would you?" Nash asked.

At that, Patterson delivered a backhand across Nash's mouth, splitting his lip. "Where's the fucking tape?"

"I dropped it."

"I don't think you understand what's happening here," Patterson said.

"Nash, don't. It's not worth it," Escobar said. After putting his clothes back on, he had moved to a bench in a far corner of the room. As he stepped forward now to intervene on Nash's behalf, laboring for every breath, Escobar looked like a man who had found himself on the Moon without a space suit.

"Stay out of this, Curt," Patterson said. "You'll get your turn."

Nash appealed to Officer Jeff. "Can't you see he needs a doctor?"

"He might be right," Jeff said, watching as Escobar sat back down on the bench.

"I thought I told you to shut the hell up," Patterson said, grabbing the Taser off the table. "How would you like a taste of your own medicine?"

"All right, all right," Jeff said. "Just get this over with."

"Sure," Patterson said, putting the stun gun down. He grabbed the collar of Nash's T-shirt and tore it in half with one yank.

For such a strung-out guy, Patterson was surprisingly strong when he was flying, Nash thought as the officer looked in what remained of the shirt pocket.

"Do a cavity check on him," Patterson said, pushing Nash toward the examining table. "And don't grease the glove."

The search was painful, but Nash bit his tongue and thought of revenge.

"He's clean," Jeff said after almost a full minute.

Nash wondered if he saw the irony in his statement.

Jeff peeled off the gloves and tossed them in the trash can, where they landed on the handle of the baton.

"You're better than oat bran," Nash said, pulling his pants back on.

Patterson paced across the room, then stopped abruptly. "Don't tell me you hid the tape in your cast," he said, shaking his head.

"We can X-ray it," Jeff volunteered.

"Oh, I don't know," Patterson said, walking over to grab Nash's wrist, "I'd kind of like to go the old-fashioned route." He turned Nash around and placed the cast on the steel examining table. "Hold this a second for me," he said in a threatening tone.

As Jeff held the arm in place, Patterson grabbed the stick back out of the trash can, scraping the gloves off on the rim. "Now let's see what kind of prizes we have in this *piñata*."

The table vibrated for several seconds after the first blow. The cast showed a long, lateral crack. The second shot shattered the plaster into chunks of dust. The force of the impact made Nash's arm go numb below the elbow.

"Where is it?" Patterson yelled.

Nash flexed his pale arm, trying to bring some life back into it. Although the wrist was now more tender than ever, the blows had landed mostly on Nash's arm. The bones didn't seem to be re-broken.

"That's enough," Jeff said, stepping forward.

"He's got it hid somewhere," Patterson pleaded.

"I don't care if he's got tomorrow's lottery number," Jeff said. "Get the hell out of my office before I call in the lieutenant." He was pointing the Taser at Patterson's chest. "And if I hear these prisoners were beaten in their cells, I'll report everything I've seen here."

Sitting in the dark, hot cell, Nash tried to puzzle out everything that had happened.

Obviously, Carr and Snipes had been able to set aside their differences long enough to deal with a common threat. Nash was glad the arrest set-up had provided them an opportunity to get Escobar out of the way without killing him. But that was a small victory in light of the fact they all might end up dead after the arms shipment was safely out of the country. Either that, or they'd rot in jail on attempted murder charges.

But it still didn't add up. Calling in Patterson had been a desperate move. If Nash and Escobar were allowed to communicate at all with the outside world after the shipment, Carr had to know they would come out with the entire story. They had simply stirred up the shit too much to leave Carr with an unclouded future.

But, logically, if Carr and Snipes were going to kill them, they would have done it right at the drive-in, he thought. The fact they were being held in solitary suggested Carr and Snipes would be accompanying the arms shipment out of the country, probably to someplace with no extradition agreement with the United States.

Nash considered Carr's story at the shooting range and what Shane Littlefeather's wife had said about the meeting between Reese Stevens, Spice Warren, Carr, and Snipes. He had to believe her version, that they were all in on the deal together from the beginning, with Warren probably getting a one-time payoff as his end of the deal when the construction was finished.

But then something had happened. Maybe Carr's old buddy Stevens had tried to double-cross him again, just as he had with the used-car lot in the fifties. Stevens might have tried blackmailing him out of the deal, threatening to expose Carr's connection with the Four Oaks if he didn't just settle for his lucrative free real estate deal.

After all, Stevens and Snipes weren't exactly local fixtures. It would be easy enough for them to leave town if the authorities turned up the heat, and Warren could always feign ignorance and get off with a fine. But not Carr. He had made his life in San Bernardino, and his name was now linked inextricably with the Star-Time. He couldn't afford to scuttle the arms deal because he almost certainly would be implicated in the ensuing investigation.

Mexican standoff indeed. But Carr hadn't been content to shut up and take the property deal and the payoffs. He didn't want to expose Snipes and Stevens, but he could threaten them. And that was when Nash had come in. Carr's setting of the trap must have started some rather ticklish negotiations between the polished real estate developer and the violent survivalist theater manager. When Nash began poking around the Star-Time, Snipes must have thought he was there to pass along the message that Carr might get over his fear of exposing them if he wasn't cut in on the deal.

He scratched at the dead skin on his left arm and tried to finish the puzzle. After it had become apparent that Nash and Escobar were on their trail, Carr had tried to cover his back by ruining Nash's reputation, while Snipes had taken a more direct route with Escobar.

Although he'd had to have Littlefeather killed, more murders probably didn't sit well with Carr, Nash figured. Each one would be harder to cover up, and each one could mean ten cold fingers pointing the cops straight at his door. So Carr had convinced Snipes and Stevens to hold Escobar while he tried to figure out a solution, and then, when the shit had hit the fan full force, he must have decided a change of scenery would be preferable to filling up the Von's Dumpster with bodies.

If his assessment was accurate, he needed to get out of jail tonight, Nash thought. By tomorrow afternoon, Carr, Snipes, and Stevens would be on their way to Brazil or South Africa. He might be able to drop the hammer on Klete Patterson, maybe even on Spice Warren, but if the three ringleaders were out of the law's reach, no one would ever have to answer for the murders of Shane Littlefeather and the Miller family.

Nash hoped Carl Barns had photographed the incident at the Star-Time from his rooftop nest and that he'd somehow find a way to get a lawyer in contact with him, or with Escobar. If Escobar was still alive.

Chapter Twenty-seven

At ten-thirty that evening, the door to Nash's cell swung open and a sour-looking guard motioned for him to step outside.

"Don't tell me I'm getting the chair," Nash said.

Never saying a word, the guard let out Homer and Escobar, then led them all down the long hallway to the outside world. Escobar was so weak that Homer and Nash had to hold him up while they walked. His shirt was soaked with fever sweat and he was gasping and wheezing like a busted fireplace bellows.

"I think I'm going to have to miss tonight's double feature," Escobar whispered to Nash as the guard called for the main door to be opened.

"I'll let you know how it turns out."

When Nash saw Carl Barns standing in front of the guard station, he sent him to call for an ambulance.

"Meet you out front in five minutes," Nash said as the photographer headed for a pay phone down the hall.

After depositing Escobar on a bench just inside the front door, Nash went back to the main desk to retrieve the tape of his conversation with Klete Patterson. He peered under the overhanging ledge, but the room's dim lighting made it hard to tell which blob of gum hid the microcassette. After running his hands over at least a dozen hard mounds, Nash glanced down at the floor and spotted the tape sitting about six inches in front of the counter, where it had apparently fallen after coming unstuck. He scooped it up, amazed that no one had stepped on it.

"Excuse me," Nash said to the desk sergeant. A man in his mid-fifties, he was checking out yesterday's results from Santa Anita in the *Racing Form*.

"How can I help you?" he mumbled in monotone without glancing up.

"I'm looking for Officer Patterson."

"He went home hours ago." The sergeant turned the page and slapped the desk in surprise. "I'll be damned. Sultan of Swat in the seventh. I didn't think that old bag of bones had it in him."

As Nash turned to leave, he saw Carl come running down the station's main corridor. The contents of his vest pockets could be heard jingling thirty feet away.

"It's on the way," Carl yelled.

Nash gave him a thumb's up and pointed towards the entrance.

They found Escobar stretched out on the bench with his left arm over his eyes. His lips were blue.

"Curt?" Nash asked, hoping he hadn't passed out.

"Would somebody please shoot me now?" Escobar whispered.

"You shouldn't talk like that in a place like this," Nash said. "Besides, the ambulance is on its way."

Just then, Homer came loping up. "I tried to get the Redhawk, but they said they couldn't release it to me without a license," he said.

"Carl, you wouldn't happen to be hiding a pistol in one of those vest pockets, would you?" Nash asked.

"I'm not that kind of shooter."

Nash turned to Homer. "Can you get us another gun?"

"I think so. The Angels stop in at the same honky-tonk for a few beers almost every night."

"All right. Go with Carl and find all the firepower you can; I'm going to make sure Escobar gets checked into the hospital all right. Meet me outside the Star-Time at midnight."

"We can take my car," Carl said.

"By the way, how did you come up with our bail so fast?" Nash asked.

"What bail? You were never officially booked into this fine facility. If I hadn't seen what happened at the drive-in, you guys could have been hidden in here for days."

"Did you bribe somebody?"

"More like blackmail," Carl said. "I got some great shots of that cop roughing you up, and ignoring the guys with the Uzis. Then I went to the chief's house and interrupted his supper to show him the prints. I told him we were going page one with the worst ones tomorrow unless he got you guys out tonight. He seemed pretty upset about the whole incident; I think this cop was acting on his own."

"That's the impression I got when they searched us," Nash said.

"Do you have a plan for tonight's action, or are we just going to barge in like we did this afternoon?" Homer asked.

"Right now, Carr, Snipes and Reese Stevens think we're still in jail," Nash said. "And they can't very well load up the weapons at the Star-Time while the second feature's going on. They'll have to wait until the last car leaves at about twelve-thirty, which gives us enough time to get in position to bring them down."

"That sounds promising," Homer said.

★ ★ ★ ★ ★

As Carl opened the door to leave, the ambulance arrived and three paramedics rushed up the police department steps carrying a collapsible stretcher. Within forty-five seconds, they had Escobar secured and at the curb. Watching him being loaded into the wagon, Nash realized that his condition had worsened considerably during the wait.

When they saw Nash's wrist, the paramedics told him to come along for treatment. As the ambulance started up, Escobar tried to whisper, but Nash could hear only a deep rattling coming from his throat. He leaned in close so that his friend's lips were almost touching his ear.

"If I die, I want you to kill that bastard Klete," Escobar said, grabbing onto Nash's left sleeve as he began to cough. "And Malcolm Snipes, too."

"Is there anyone I should call to come sit with you?"

"No," Escobar whispered. "I'm alone."

"You need to sit off to the side while we help your friend," a paramedic told Nash.

Escobar was unconscious now and Nash couldn't tell if he was breathing. The paramedics moved efficiently around the back of the ambulance, one securing an oxygen mask over Escobar's face while the other inserted a saline drip into his left arm.

The youngest paramedic listened to Escobar's lungs through a stethoscope, looked up at his partner and shook his head. "No breath sounds on the right side," he said.

"Could be full of fluid," said the other one, so tall he had to bend almost in half to avoid bumping his head on the roof.

"Looks like we'll have to Ambu-bag him."

Nash took a step forward for a better view. "What's that?" he asked, pointing at the black plastic bulb and the long, flexible tube the tall one had pulled out of a cabinet. The bulb looked like the kind photographers used to use for tripod shots, except bigger.

The young one pushed Nash back to his original spot with his left hand while he removed Escobar's oxygen mask with his right.

"We're preparing to intubate your friend," said the tall one as he stripped the plastic wrapping off the tube. "It looks like his right lung has been punctured and we're sticking this endo-trachial here down into it. We'll cap the tube with this bag and squeeze it to help get him breathing again."

They worked quickly, one holding Escobar's mouth open, while the other snaked the tube down his throat. The young paramedic pressed the Ambu-bag onto the endo-trachial tube and started forcing air into the collapsed lung. On the third squeeze, Escobar began coughing, sending a stream of blood up through the clear tube and into the bag.

"Holy shit," Nash said.

"We're into some heavy fluid down there," the tall paramedic said. "Probably been building up for a while."

The blood streaming out of the tube reminded Nash of a deep, murky river running fast with spring run-off.

A perfect spot for one of Evan Carr's drowning sets.

When the ambulance pulled up to the hospital three minutes later, the blood had slowed to a trickle and Escobar's lips were no longer blue.

"We're putting him back on oxygen for the trip inside," the tall one said. "He's pretty well cleaned out now and we've got air into that right lung again."

The paramedics eased the stretcher onto the pavement, the driver holding up the IV bag, and then moved quickly toward the emergency room.

"I've seen a lot worse than this," the young one said to Nash as they wheeled Escobar through the automatic doors. "He's gonna make it."

After Escobar was taken away for X-rays, Nash tried to think of who he could call to look in on Curt later. It would have to be someone who knew them both and who didn't want Nash's head on a platter. It would have to be Faye Krashenko, the features editor.

Nash borrowed a phone book from the emergency room receptionist and looked up her number. It was listed under Krashenko, F. As he dialed, he wondered if she was seriously interested in Curt. He decided to leave that for Escobar to find out.

"Hello," said Faye Krashenko. He heard the noise of the TV in the background.

"Hi, this is Nash Hansen. I hope I didn't wake you."

"Are you kidding? Not when George Clooney's on Letterman. But what the hell are you calling me for? I thought you left town under mysterious circumstances."

"I'm working undercover. It's related to the drive-in story."

"Remodeled theaters must be more exciting than I thought."

"I'm sorry I didn't finish the feature."

"No problem," Faye said. "I just ran a wire-service piece on the shifting focus of culture in Southern California. It seems we're moving from shopping malls to big discount stores. We'll probably have to open a Wal-Mart bureau."

"Faye, Curt Escobar has been working on this investigation with me. He's hurt pretty bad."

"That's terrible."

"I'm glad you feel that way. I need you to do him a favor."

"Name it."

"Curt's about to go into surgery for a collapsed lung. I'd like to be there when he gets out, but I've got to be back at the Star-Time in about an hour."

"And you thought I'd be an appropriate substitute?"

"Yes. He's at San Bernardino General."

"I'm touched," Faye said. "I'll be there."

"One more request?"

"Shoot."

"Bring Twinkies."

Escobar was awake and back from X-ray when Nash returned to the emergency room. A nurse told him the anesthesiologist was on her way. As soon as she arrived, they would take Escobar in for surgery.

"Hey buddy," Nash said, leaning in close to the stretcher.

"Why aren't you out kicking ass?" Escobar whispered.

"Soon, Curt. Faye Krashenko's on her way down here to hold your hand until I get done with Snipes and Carr. I forgot to tell you the other day, she's been wanting to spend more time with you."

"Way to go, Rambler."

Fifteen minutes after Escobar was wheeled into the operating room, Faye Krashenko arrived. Not only did she bring a box of Twinkies, she insisted on letting Nash drive her Saab to the Star-Time.

"I won't be using it until you get back here anyway," she said. "Nash, you really look like shit. Come here."

When she hugged him, Nash realized he hadn't taken a deep, easy breath in several days. He rested his head on Faye's shoulder, and he felt like he was floating. The moorings of death, betrayal, and hatred that had been tying him down fell away as he rose, and he wanted only to sleep and float through the clouds.

A twinge of pain in his left wrist brought him back down to earth. In the rush to plan the raid on the Star-Time and get Escobar to the hospital, he had forgotten about Patterson destroying his cast, and the paramedics had understandably concentrated on Curt. If he asked for assistance, Nash knew he would be stuck filling out forms, sitting for X-rays, and waiting for plaster to dry, but he didn't want to face Snipes and Carr without protecting his arm. He wanted to find an Ace bandage at least.

With Faye standing guard, Nash stepped into an empty treatment station, drew the curtain, and began opening drawers. The third one yielded a box of air splints. He fastened the Velcro strips and blew up the plastic sleeve until he could no longer flex his wrist. The splint wasn't as sturdy as he would have hoped, but it would do.

As he drove across town to the theater, Nash thought about the request Escobar had made in the ambulance. Was he ready to take another man's life if Curt didn't make it? Snipes had done him a lot of damage, and Klete Patterson was nothing but bad news, but Nash wasn't sure if he could bring himself to kill either of them, even in self-defense. That was one of the reasons he had gone into reporting instead of police work. He wanted to help put away murderers and thieves, but he didn't think he had the right to rub them out.

Maybe his mind-set had changed a little when he had learned of the Miller family's murder and the hit Carr had ordered on Shane Littlefeather. Maybe he had become just a bit more fed up when Carr had double-crossed him and Klete Patterson had punctured Escobar's lung at the drive-in and then threw him in solitary to die. Maybe he wouldn't have such a problem killing a man who would help fuel a war just to pad his bank account.

Pulling into the circular drive of the Star-Time, Nash knew it was time to find out.

The plastic sleeve of the air splint was making his wrist sweat, so Nash unrolled the window of the Saab and stuck his left arm into the light breeze that was rolling through the valley. As he held up his right arm to try to make out the dial of his watch, he heard the snick of a rifle bolt being pulled back.

He turned to see Malcolm Snipes looking down at him over the barrel of an assault rifle.

"I told Carr we'd have to get rid of you sooner or later," Snipes said. He was dressed all in black, but his teeth picked up the glow of a halogen street lamp when he smiled. "And I, for one, am gonna enjoy it."

Chapter Twenty-eight

Following Snipes' instructions, Nash got out of the car and walked around the front to climb in the passenger side. Snipes eased himself behind the wheel, the battered M1 carbine in his lap almost touching Nash's stomach, and drove behind the snack bar of the Star-Time.

"Concession stand always closes a half-hour before the end of the last show," Snipes said as he led Nash into the small concrete building. "We've got the place to ourselves."

Closing the door behind him, Snipes flipped on the lights and gestured for Nash to keep moving toward the back of the room. The theater manager followed him into the office and opened a large trap door behind the desk. A metal ladder descended into a well-lit warehouse area. Snipes gestured for Nash to climb down.

The scene that greeted him when he hit the floor was disconcerting. Instead of armed thugs with watch caps and grease on their faces, perhaps fifty trailer-park people, entire families in their Sunday best, milled about the huge basement area, chatting, sipping coffee from Styrofoam cups, and eating homemade cake and cookies. Some of the children, older boys mostly, were running around the support pillars at the far end of the room and shooting at each other with toy guns.

Besides the numerous barrels of water and boxes of weapons, army Meals Ready to Eat, radiation detectors, medical supplies, and toilet paper stacked in neat towers along every wall, the room included a makeshift chapel complete with several dozen metal folding chairs, an urn of holy water, and a dark wood pulpit. The milling crowd apparently was waiting for evening services to begin.

As Snipes prodded him toward the chapel area, Nash noticed several open boxes of gas masks and heavy cloth jumpsuits sitting just behind the pulpit next to a tall, silver canister.

"Is that the hydrogen selenide gas you stole?"

Snipes seemed surprised at the question. "How did you know about that?"

"I read it in the *Ledger*."

As they neared a pile of hymnals, a man in a clerical collar finished up a conversation with a group of parishioners near the coffee urn and walked over to meet Snipes.

"Is this another friend from the fourth estate?" the preacher asked. He was in his mid-sixties, about six-five, taller than everyone in his congregation. He sported a helmet of moussed brown hair and he had added a few extra years to his face in pursuit of a deep, permanent tan. In short, he looked like a perennial candidate for office.

"I'm Nash Hansen." He held out his hand to the preacher. "You must be the noted swindler, embezzler, and arms merchant, Reese Stevens."

"He has as much of a sense of humor as his friend Escobar," Stevens said, completing the handshake. "It's too bad he won't be around to amuse us after tonight's service."

"So, your flock does the heavy lifting and provides your operation with a steady cash flow between arms deals with Latin American dictators?" Nash asked.

"I wouldn't put it quite that way," Stevens replied. "But essentially, you are correct. Members of the Four Oaks work together toward several common goals: preserving democracy in our hemisphere, promoting decent family values here at home, and providing ourselves with a sanctuary from the coming Armageddon that will wipe the sinners from the face of the earth. The parishioners you see here tonight are simply concerned, patriotic Americans."

"Sounds like great copy for a promotional brochure."

"I believe very strongly in the principles of the Four Oaks," Stevens said, dropping the amiable smile.

"Is that why you plan to leave the country with Carr and Mr. Snipes here as soon as the shipment passes over the border?"

"We have no such plans. Why would we leave when we have such a secure sanctuary and so many people dedicated to our cause?"

"If you were going to stay, Carr never would have allowed me and Escobar to leave the drive-in alive today. You only wanted us held until you could skip town."

The smile, which had reappeared briefly, again vanished from Reese Stevens' face. "Believe what you wish," he said. "I only hope your theories provide you some solace on your journey to hell."

"Where's Evan Carr?" Nash asked. "Home packing up his collection of traps? Or maybe he's already gone."

"You're awfully curious for a dead man, Mr. Hansen," Stevens replied. "Malcolm, won't you make our friend comfortable while I gather up my flock?"

With that, Snipes led Nash to the nearest support pillar and lashed him to it with cotton rope. He had a clear view of the congregation and he watched as, one by one, they passed behind the pulpit to pick up a hymnal, a jumpsuit, and a gas mask on their way to the makeshift pews. He was beginning to wonder what was taking Homer and Carl Barns so long.

He hoped they weren't caught up in the exciting climax of the second feature.

Soon, Reese Stevens stepped up to the pulpit and opened a worn, leather-bound Bible. The parishioners sat primly with the hymnals and jumpsuits on their laps; the gas masks hung loosely around their necks. Malcolm Snipes wrestled the canister of hydrogen selenide into view and found a seat in the front row.

Nash thought of the article on the canister's theft and its description of the painful death that awaited anyone breathing its contents. He remembered something about the gas destroying the lungs, liver, and spleen of those who came in contact with it. It would be a colorless, odorless, utterly hideous, death.

In rising tones, Stevens began to deliver his sermon:

"Friends, in just a few hours we will realize the fruit of the labors we have undertaken these past several months. When this special service ends, three moving vans will arrive and we will begin loading the arsenal of freedom that you see before you. The weapons will then be transported to our desert landing strip where they will begin their long journey south to the willing and able hands of our Venezuelan allies.

"We have the godless Communists on the ropes in Russia and around the world. And with the help of this arsenal, the loyal Venezuelan government-in-waiting can depose the Marxist pretender who refuses to pledge allegiance to the forces of freedom and justice."

As the story began to fall into place, Nash's desire for a tape recorder almost eclipsed his fear of death by gas.

"Our government would like to do this job for us," Stevens continued. "But in this particular instance, our leaders are in a bind. The most recent attempt to restore order in Venezuela failed, the Marxist dictator was restored to power, and other Latin nations accused our president of trying to undermine a 'democratically elected government.' So for now, America's hands are tied. But ours remain free to do God's work.

"The Four Oaks and several like-minded groups are providing the anti-Communist forces with critical military hardware in a covert fashion. And I am here to tell you that several of our nation's law-enforcement agencies have graciously seen fit to turn a blind eye to our patriotic activities. So, while you may not receive any medals for the work you have done here, rest assured that a grateful nation secretly thanks you for doing your part to keep the Western Hemisphere secure for true democracy."

Pausing to wipe his brow with a white, monogrammed handkerchief, Stevens began to read aloud from the Bible. Judging from the appreciative murmurs of the flock, it was a favorite selection.

" 'But the Lord is with me as a dread warrior; therefore my persecutors will stumble, they will not overcome me'," he intoned.

" 'They will be greatly shamed, for they will not succeed.

" 'Their eternal dishonor will not be forgotten.

" 'O Lord of hosts, who triest the righteous, who seest the heart and the mind, let me see thy vengeance upon them, for to thee have I committed my cause.' "

"Amen," cried several parishioners. One, overcome with emotion, began speaking in tongues.

Stevens closed the well-worn book and led the assembly in a rousing rendition of "Bringing in the Sheaves." As the words echoed eerily off the far walls, Nash felt a bout of claustrophobia coming on. He closed his eyes and tried to picture himself running along a beach, his bare feet sending up sprays of surf. But the more he tried not to think about being tied up, the more he felt the rough concrete pillar digging into his back and the rings of thick cotton rope squeezing him like hungry boa constrictors.

With his breath coming in shorter gasps, he had to find a way to curb his panic attack. If he was going to die, he at least wanted to go out on an even keel. Nash turned his head and noticed a knot in the rope near his left arm. Curling his fingers into the palm of his hand, he touched the pumped-up air sleeve of the plastic splint. If he could release the air, he reasoned, he might be able to undo the cast and slip his hand out to untie the rope.

Nash began digging his fingernails into the soft bladder. As he focused on the arduous task, he was able to partially block out his fear. His breathing was returning to normal and his muscles were starting to relax when Stevens spoke again.

"It is now time to test our defenses against a chemical attack," the preacher said. "When the Armageddon comes, radiation and nerve gas will be our two worst enemies. We must be prepared to battle them as if they were the very forces of Satan and darkness."

Stevens raised his head to the concrete ceiling, his hands outstretched, and asked his flock, "Do you believe?"

"Yes," the parishioners chanted, their response reverberating throughout the room. Nash prayed that someone would hear them shouting. He continued trying to puncture the air bladder, but his breathing again came in short, sharp bursts.

"I'm glad to hear you say that," Stevens continued. "Because during our last test, one of the families among us didn't believe. They refused to put their trust in the Lord, and He punished them. We all watched them writhe in agony when

God in His infinite wisdom saw fit to smite them down for their sins.

"They did not believe. They wanted to leave the flock. As a result, every breath they took brought vile poison into their lungs, even though they were outfitted with the same masks you wear around your necks today. I am especially sorrowful that the little girl was forced to forfeit her tender young soul to pay for the blasphemy of her parents, but we must heed the Lord's message so that she will not have died in vain.

"We must remember that message as it is written in the Book of Proverbs: 'For a man's ways are before the eyes of the Lord and he watches all his paths. The iniquities of the wicked ensnare him, and he is caught in the toils of sin. He dies for lack of discipline, and because of his great folly he is lost.'

"I ask you then, brothers and sisters: Do you believe?"

The flock thundered once more and Nash, his fingers cramping up, gave one final push on the air sleeve.

"I say: Do you believe?"

The nail of Nash's index finger drove past the plastic and he felt the air escape through the hole.

"In the name of God Almighty, Do you believe?"

With the extra inch of space afforded him by the deflated bladder, Nash wriggled out of the splint. His wrist sang with pain as he slowly worked his left arm to the top of the rope. The chanting of the flock had reached a fever pitch and Malcolm Snipes was stepping up to the canister of gas.

"Everyone!" Reese Stevens bellowed. "Fasten your masks and put on your chemical suits. We are on a thirty-second drill. Deacon Snipes, are you ready?"

Snipes nodded as he and Stevens fitted their gas masks and protective headgear into place. There was a frenzy of activity in the pews as parishioners frantically kicked over folding chairs and began stepping into the hooded, olive-green jumpsuits.

Suddenly, Nash's arm popped free of the rope and he began working hard on the knot, his fingers going numb as searing pain shot up from his wrist all the way to his shoulder. Snipes looked his way as he put a hand on the valve of the aluminum canister. The theater manager pointed him out to Stevens, and Nash realized he wouldn't have time to work free before the hydrogen selenide began to seep out of the tank.

As Snipes prepared to crank the valve, Nash heard a thud behind him, followed by a gunshot, more thuds, and shouting. The bullet hit Reese Stevens in the shoulder, tearing open his chemical suit and spinning him backward in the process.

"Malcolm, wait," Stevens shouted as he fell. "Don't open the tank." Snipes backed away from the canister and crouched down in the front row to retrieve his rifle.

"Nash," Homer yelled as he ran up to the column with Carl Barns. About a dozen armed Berdoo Angels followed close behind.

"Be careful where you shoot," Nash said. "This place is full of poison gas and explosives." Turning to his left, he saw the Angel with the butterfly knife cutting through his ropes.

"Snipes has an assault rifle," Carl shouted as Homer went down on his knees and took aim with a sawed-off shotgun. Freed from his bonds, Nash dropped to the ground and rolled behind a barrel of water as Snipes stood up and cranked off several rounds in their direction.

Unfazed and unhit, Homer pulled back the hammers and let loose with both barrels, cutting Snipes down at the knees. Falling forward into a pile of folding chairs, the manager shot several wild rounds into a stack of radiation detectors.

"Watch out for the kids," Nash said as Homer reloaded the shotgun. In the confusion, many of the parishioners had scrambled for cover and grabbed weapons from the surrounding crates, but several of the younger children sat in the open, crying and frozen with terror.

"Let's get the hell out of here," Homer said when several members of the flock began returning fire. As the Angels ran for cover behind the pillars at the back of the basement, Butterfly Knife caught a slug in his right thigh, which sent him sprawling in the middle of an open area.

"Cover me," Homer said, tossing Nash a .45 automatic as he doubled back to pull the fallen Angel to safety. Nash edged behind a crate of government rations and helped four of the bikers lay down a shaky crossfire in front of Butterfly Knife.

But as Homer started pulling Butterfly to cover, Reese Stevens emerged from behind a wall of crates about twenty-five feet away and began blasting at them with his assault rifle. Several shots found their mark and Homer let go of the Angel with a groan. The noise of the bullets ricocheting around the basement had reached a deafening pitch and Nash felt disoriented and dizzy as he returned Stevens' fire.

"Get him, Nash," Homer said as he started crawling away from the killing zone. Blood was splattered all over his shirt and pants legs and Nash couldn't tell how much of it was from Butterfly's wound and how much of it was coming from Homer. He only knew he had to stop Stevens, now.

Wheeling out into the open, he shouted "Hey!" and momentarily caught the preacher's eye. In Stevens' moment of hesitation, Nash steadied himself and unloaded the rest of the .45's magazine into the preacher's body. The assault rifle clattered to the ground and Stevens crumpled over it, dead.

Throwing away the empty pistol, Nash ran out into the open with Carl to retrieve Homer and Butterfly as the other Angels continued to lay down suppressing fire. Soon, they had pulled back to the ladder and the shooting from the other end of the room had subsided.

"Hold it," Snipes yelled. From his position on the floor, he had grabbed a young child. He held her close, pressing a pistol against her temple. "Anyone leaves this basement and she dies."

The Angels stopped and turned to face the flock, but as they did, a single shot rang out from behind the overturned pulpit.

"Come here, honey," a woman said, dropping the pistol she had used to shoot Snipes in the back of the head. "That mean man isn't going to hurt you anymore."

As the girl ran into her mother's arms, two Angels helped Carl Barns hoist Homer and Butterfly Knife up the ladder. They were both still breathing. Nash's wrist was so tender that another biker had to help him climb out of the basement.

As they entered the deserted theater lot, Nash borrowed a .38 from his old pal Skull Bong and instructed him to drive the wounded Angels to the hospital in Faye Krashenko's Saab and then call the cops about the mess downstairs.

"Maybe you should go with them," Carl said. "That wrist doesn't look so good."

"Did you drive?" Nash asked.

"Yeah," the photographer said, pointing to his Plymouth. "Want me to take you to General?"

"No. We've got to get to Carr's house before he skips town."

I just killed a man, Nash thought as he climbed into the passenger seat. He hoped Evan Carr wouldn't demand a repeat performance.

Chapter Twenty-nine

Evan Carr lived in an iron-fenced, two-acre compound that butted against the foothills northwest of town. When Nash and Carl Barns arrived at the main gate, it was almost two A.M., but numerous lights were still on in the main house. Nash grabbed one of Carl's telephoto lenses and watched as several servants loaded boxes into a small moving van parked at the head of the drive. Through the open front door, he could see Carr directing traffic and talking on the phone.

"Looks like our man's been tipped off," Nash said.

"It's his home turf and we've lost the element of surprise," Carl replied. "What do you suggest?"

Nash hefted the lens in his hand and thought for a moment. "Do you have any lighting equipment with you?"

"Always. Why?"

"I think it's time to stage the ultimate ambush interview."

With Nash's help, Carl pulled six battery-powered, remote-controlled light poles out of the trunk and rigged them up just outside the gate on either side of the drive. Each lamp was outfitted with a 500-watt halogen bulb.

As the loading of the moving van slowed to a trickle of boxes, Carr grabbed his briefcase and walked onto the front porch to signal his driver. The white Mercedes came around the side of the house and Carr stepped inside. The electronic gates began to open as the car made its way down the fifty-yard drive. Holding the .38 Skull Bong had given him, Nash crouched in the shadow of a palm tree while the photographer waited behind the open door of his Plymouth just down the road.

"Now!" Nash yelled when the Mercedes started through the gate.

Carl pressed the remote button and flashed three thousand watts of pure, white light into the driver's eyes, causing him to swerve onto the curb and stop. Nash pumped two rounds into the left front tire of the Mercedes and shouted for Carr to get out, but there was no response from inside. The three servants at the moving van had started to run down the driveway at the sound of the gunshots. Watching them approach, Nash knew he didn't have much time to pull this off.

Moving to the front of the Mercedes, he raised the .38 and took aim at the tinted windshield.

"If you're not going to get out, you'd better duck," Nash said. He pulled the trigger and sent a shower of safety glass into the air. The driver opened the door and rolled out, but Carr had dived down in the back seat and made no move to leave. The servants were almost at the gate, and Nash was becoming frustrated. "Do I have to kill you to get you out of there?"

"Drop it," the driver said as he came up with his service pistol aimed at Nash's chest. It was Klete Patterson.

"We heard you might be coming our way," Patterson said, waving back the concerned servants.

Nash dropped the gun and Evan Carr poked his head above the front seat. As soon as Patterson bent over to pick up the .38, Carl Barns floored the Plymouth backwards down the road.

"Shit," Patterson said as Carl disappeared around a corner.

"Let him go," Carr said. He climbed out of the Mercedes,

smoothed the jacket of his tan cotton summer suit and pulled out a pistol of his own, an automatic.

"Off to sun-drenched climes?" Nash asked.

"I gave you a chance to live even though you've single-handedly forced me to leave my home of sixty-four years," Carr said. "Yes, I got a call from the drive-in. You've ruined my good name, killed my associates, and cost me a great deal of money. I'll be lucky to get out of the country tonight with a million dollars. That's a fraction of what I'm worth. Do you understand that you've ruined my life?"

"Just like you ruined Shane Littlefeather's?"

For a moment, Carr's shoulders slumped, but a jolt of righteous anger stiffened him up again. "That was different. Shane was threatening to expose me, just like you did. I am not a violent man by nature, but that greedy savage left me no choice."

"Who pulled the trigger for you on that job? Was it Snipes?"

Carr nodded slowly and then motioned for Patterson to bring down another car from the house. "I wish poor Malcolm were still with us," Carr said as the cop jogged up the drive. "He was insane, certainly, but he was chemical-free, unlike our friend there. I find Officer Patterson to be highly unreliable muscle. Still, I imagine he'll be up to the task of finishing you off."

"Are you sure you won't let me file one last story, for old times' sake?" Nash asked.

"I'd love to," Carr replied, smiling. "But I'm on such a tight schedule. My trap collection and I are due at a landing strip in the Mojave in under two hours. The Cayman Islands beckon."

"Then why not get this over with and kill me yourself? I'd hate to throw off your schedule." Nash took a step toward

Carr and lowered his hands. If he was going to make something happen, it would have to be before Klete Patterson returned.

"Don't try me," Carr said, steadying the 9mm Beretta with his left hand.

"Maybe you don't want to kill me in front of your neighbors." Nash nodded toward the row of houses across the street. In the past few minutes, lights had been turned on in several of them, and more than one curtain had been drawn back by residents awakened by the earlier gunshots.

"It would be pretty bad form if the cops just happened to show up while you were bending over my corpse with a smoking gun in your hand." Nash took another step forward.

"What's going on over there?" a man yelled from a yard across the street. When Carr turned his head, Nash reached out and knocked away the Beretta. They both dove for the gun, but Nash was quicker than the old man.

"This isn't like the fur trade," he said as he turned the weapon on Carr. "You're not dealing with a defenseless animal here." The growl of Carr's Porsche startled them both, and they turned to watch Klete Patterson come down the drive.

"Get in the Mercedes or I'll blow your head off," Nash said to Carr as he moved into the center of the lane. He held his fire until the Porsche was only a few yards from the gate, then he emptied the Beretta's entire clip into the driver's side of the windshield. The sports car swerved momentarily, but then bore down on him again. At the last second, Nash leapt onto the hood of the disabled Mercedes. As the Porsche slid by, he saw Patterson slumped over the steering wheel.

Patterson slammed down on the gas pedal as he died, and the car careened across the street, plowed through a chain-link fence, and crashed into the picture window of a house before coming to a stop with its back wheels spinning three feet off the ground.

Nash waited silently with Evan Carr as the wailing sirens of several squad cars and an ambulance drew closer. He felt incredibly tired, but he couldn't wait to visit Homer and Escobar at the hospital—and then sit down at the nearest computer.

Soon, the servants came back down the drive and looked to their boss for answers, but Carr didn't seem to notice. He looked out of the Mercedes' shattered windshield, blinking rapidly into the bright lights. When a young officer cuffed him and put him in a squad car five minutes later, Carr didn't resist or say a word.

"I met these cops on their way up and told them what happened," Carl said, opening the passenger door of the Plymouth. "They want you down at the station in the morning to file a report."

Nash climbed into the car slowly, closing his eyes as his head hit the seat back.

Chapter Thirty

They found Faye Krashenko reading a three-month-old *Vogue* in the San Bernardino General waiting room. When she looked up and saw Nash, she jumped to her feet.

"Thank God you're alive," she said. "When that group of bikers came in here from the drive-in, I thought World War III had been declared. Are you hurt?"

"I'll be fine as soon as a doctor looks at this." Nash held up his left wrist for Faye's inspection. It was nearly as swollen and purple as it had been the day it was broken.

"Christ."

"How's Escobar?"

"He got out of surgery an hour ago. He's still sleeping, but the doctor told me he'll be up and eating Twinkies in a few days."

Nash pumped his right fist at his side, a wave of pure joy breaking through the haze of exhaustion. "Did you see what happened to the bikers?"

"The two who were shot, do you know them?" Faye asked.

He nodded and braced for the worst.

"One of them didn't make it."

"Because the hoods who brought them in ran away rather suddenly, we did not get a positive ID on either gentleman," the emergency room receptionist said. "One of them is in surgery right now for multiple gunshot wounds. The other man has been transported to the morgue."

"Where is that?" Nash asked.

"We cannot allow unauthorized personnel in the morgue, sir. But if you come back tomorrow morning when we're fully staffed, someone will be on duty to escort you there."

"One of those men is a friend of mine. Both of them saved my life."

"I'm sorry," she said. "You'll have to wait."

"Thanks for understanding." Nash turned from the desk and walked out into the parking lot.

"You ought to have someone look at that arm," she called after him.

He found Carl Barns pacing behind a large rhododendron bush near the entrance. "How much money do you have on you?"

"Couple of twenties, I think," Carl said.

"I need to borrow one of them."

"You going to grab a sandwich?"

"No. Carl, Homer may be dead."

"Shit. Won't they tell you for sure?"

Nash shook his head. "I need to bribe someone to let me into the morgue."

"Let's go."

When the receptionist left to visit the bathroom twenty minutes later, Nash and Carl walked through the double doors leading to the bowels of the hospital. They followed the overhead signs to the morgue, hoping to run into a helpful orderly along the way.

As they made their way down the two flights of stairs to the basement, Nash thought how jarring it was to always have dispassionate professionals hovering at the fringes of the births, deaths, and weddings that were the defining moments of a person's life. Doctors, preachers, and justices of the peace. Caterers and receptionists. The crime reporter and the gossip columnist. The gravedigger and the guy who swept up the rice. For them, each joyful or heart-shattering occasion was just another day on the job.

When he had been sitting with Ronald Slasnik, the young man who'd been maimed in Evan Carr's bear trap at the Star-Time, Nash had been thinking only of the story potential of the event. Never once had it crossed his mind to see beyond the bare facts of the situation and try to understand the pain he would feel if two sets of giant, rusty teeth had slammed into his ankle with sledgehammer force, for no good reason at all.

He realized now that he had never taken a moment to feel genuine sympathy for Slasnik. The man sprawled on the gravel had been weeping with pain, his leg soaked with blood and a tray of nachos spilled around his head, and Nash had used him matter-of-factly. Just as the emergency room receptionist had so easily refused his request to see the body by throwing away her compassion and hiding behind the rules.

And, if he was going to be honest about it, just as Escobar had used the threat of exposure to hold Klete Patterson under his thumb like a bug for so many years. He thought of young Brad Lapham, who spent his free time coming up with creative ways to kill computer-animated characters, and he wondered if the concept of decency had finally gone the way of the horse-drawn cart, quaint but outmoded in a high-tech society where speed and expediency were at a premium. If that was the case, Nash thought as they approached the morgue, maybe it was time to join the Amish.

He tried the swinging doors, but they were locked.

"Maybe he's got a key," Carl said. A young custodian with his back to them about thirty feet down the corridor was mopping the floor and dancing to the loud beat of a Walkman.

When Nash walked up and tapped him on the shoulder, the startled man nearly knocked over the bucket of water. He turned on his heels and brandished the mop at Nash.

"Don't you ever do that to me again," he said. "Or I'll make you glad you're in a hospital."

Nash pulled out the twenty and tucked it into the man's shirt pocket. "We didn't mean any harm."

The janitor plucked the bill out and held it up for inspection. "Well, now that's more like it."

"But I do need to ask you a favor," Nash said.

The man looked at him and snorted. "Oh sure, anything you want."

"Look, I just need you to let me into the morgue for a minute."

"Are you serious?" The janitor studied him intently. "You're serious. What are you two, some kind of freaks or something?"

"It's nothing like that. Really. We need to identify a body."

"Uh huh. And I should lose my job just so you can get your jollies with some stiff?"

Nash thought about throwing the man against a wall, but he was sick of pissing over all of humanity to get what he needed. Instead, he got the other twenty from Carl and handed it over. "One minute," he said.

"Okay. One minute."

The room was filled with the hum of an air conditioner and the sickening sweet smell of formaldehyde. There were no bodies on the examining tables, so Nash and Carl went to opposite ends of the bank of freezer drawers and started hunting. As soon as Nash convinced himself that a body was not either Homer or Butterfly Knife, he slid the tray back in and slammed the door shut as fast as he could. But on the fifth tray, he paused. He saw someone he recognized.

It was Janie Miller, the woman from the Von's super-market Dumpster. No longer the winsome and graceful young woman from the photo he had seen in Wayne Easler's trailer, Janie was pale except for a few blotchy bruises on her neck and upper chest. Her open eyes were filled with the horror of her asphyxiation.

"Carl, does the county medical examiner work out of this hospital?"

"Yeah. They bring all the murder victims here."

"I just found Janie Miller. Snipes gassed her and her family at the Star-Time about a week ago." Nash hoped they would bury her soon.

Carl walked over and put an arm on his shoulder and eased the tray back into the freezer. "Go sit down a minute," Carl said. "I'll keep looking."

Nash went into the hall for some air. As he watched the janitor cleaning up the sudsy spill, he felt glad he hadn't opened the door on Janie Miller's daughter.

"You done in there?" the man asked.

"Almost."

As he said it, the double doors swung open and Carl gestured for Nash to come back in. A tray in the middle of the freezer bank was pulled halfway out to reveal a large form covered with a white, blood-spotted sheet. When he saw it, Nash felt a tightness in his throat.

He pulled back the sheet and, for a moment, saw Homer's eyes looking back at him. But when he took a deep breath and looked again, Nash realized his mind had tricked him into believing the worst had come true.

Butterfly Knife was laid out with his eyes closed and his arms stiff at his sides. Nash saw four bullet holes in his naked body, including one from a slug that had traveled through his back and erupted out of his chest.

Butterfly Knife, he thought bitterly. The man before him had died saving his life, and Nash didn't even know his name.

Reaching into his pocket, Nash found the wolf talisman that Homer had given him. He placed the charm on top of the sheet.

"Homer says this is powerful medicine," he said. "I hope it helps you wherever you're going."

The tightness in Nash's throat turned into choking. He pushed in the tray and let the stainless steel door swing shut behind it.

"Let's get the hell out of here," he said.

After Nash sent Carl Barns away to pick out the best shots from the drive-in, he headed down to the emergency room to be fitted with a new cast.

As soon as the plaster was set, Nash found Faye Krashenko in the waiting room. Homer was out of surgery now, too, she told him, but they'd have to wait until eight A.M. to see him and Escobar.

With the sky still dark to the East, Nash borrowed a notebook Faye had in her purse, grabbed a Diet Coke, and began lashing together a longhand first draft of the story he'd almost died reporting. After working in a few quotes and a little color from his notes, it might turn out to be a real winner, he thought.

Just before nine, Nash found Escobar's room on the third floor and entered to the sound of laughter. Faye Krashenko smiled at him from her chair next to the bed. Escobar was sitting up. He had a drainage tube in his chest and three full-size pillows wedged behind his back. "Headline News" was playing on the television, but neither of them seemed to be paying much attention to it.

"Sorry to bust in on your social club," Nash said.

"Good to see you, Rambler." Escobar's voice was still raspy, but it was louder than it had been before the surgery.

"Ditto," Nash replied.

"The doctor says his lung's going to be just fine," Faye said. She was holding Escobar's left hand. "I could have figured that out myself, though. He's been filling the room with hot air for the past twenty minutes."

"No oxygen feed?"

"Nope," she said. "The lung's intact. Sore, but intact."

"I'm okay, Rambler." Escobar pushed himself into a more comfortable position. "Did you get Carr?"

"He's in jail. And I think you should know that you're going to have to find a new source in the police department."

"Dead?"

Nash nodded.

"He deserved it," Escobar said. "Now would you please get the hell out of here and write up the story before every paper in California beats you to it?"

"Don't worry," Faye said. "I'll stay with him a while longer so he doesn't drive all the nurses crazy."

At ten, with Homer still asleep, Nash phoned Slant in Chicago to fill him in on the action.

"I called my friend at the *Orange County Register* last night," Slant said. "He's waiting to take a look at your piece."

"Thanks."

"With any luck, the wires will pick it up and give it some

national play. Then you could use it to get an assignment from any number of outlets—*Tribune*, *Times*, *Post*, you name it."

"Whoa there, Slant. Do you think I might be able to catch a few hours' sleep before you turn me into a media celebrity?"

"You can sleep when you're dead, Nash. Right now is the time to jump on this thing. Start investigating the government connection to this Venezuelan arms deal."

"Reese Stevens said in his sermon last night that the feds were taking a hands-off approach to the whole operation," Nash offered.

"But don't you find it a little odd that the FBI would lose track of this Snipes character right before he goes to bat for some of our thug-like friends to the south?" Slant asked.

"Sure. But how am I going to investigate something as big as that?"

"Just write what you have. If the feds are involved, they'll probably come to you with threats and denials, just like the White House did after Watergate. If they start squawking, you've got 'em. Then you'll have the *Post*, the *Times* and all the newsmagazines helping to dig up the bodies, not to mention the networks and CNN."

"Okay, I'm pumped up already."

"Then go do it. And when you're done with the first story, bring it to Moe Bankhead at the *Register*. Today."

As he hung up the receiver, Nash noticed the head nurse standing over his shoulder.

"Your friend's awake, Mr. Hansen. He'd like to see you."

Homer looked even worse than usual, Nash thought as he opened the door to room 306. He was practically a mass of bandages—his ear, chest, right shoulder, and left leg were all wrapped tight in white gauze and tape.

"Set off any metal detectors lately?" Nash asked as he sat down next to the bed.

A smile passed across Homer's lips, but his eyes remained deadly serious. "How's Henry doing?" he asked weakly. "They wouldn't tell me."

"Henry?"

"Yeah, Henry. The Angel who saved your life."

"I didn't know his name," Nash said, almost to himself. "Henry what?"

"Painter. Henry Painter. So how is he?"

"He's dead, Homer."

"Shit." Homer turned away and stared out into the parking lot. "Did you see him?"

"Yes. He took at least four shots. One blew out the middle of his chest."

"Jesus." After a moment, Homer turned back to face Nash. "Does his wife know?"

"The hospital didn't have a positive ID."

"Connie must be worried out of her mind."

"I wish I had known his name."

"Doesn't make much difference now, does it?"

"Yeah, it does, Homer. It really does."

Chapter Thirty-one

By noon, Nash was satisfied with the story. Two hours later, Moe Bankhead, managing editor of the *Orange County Register*, agreed to run the piece on the front page, along with three of Carl's photos. By seven, Nash had given a statement to the police, along with copies of his tape and notes. Both Evan Carr and Spice Warren, the owner of Warren Construction, were in custody, with charges pending against them under a variety of local, state, and federal statutes.

As he opened the door to his apartment at eight-thirty that evening, Nash realized he hadn't closed his eyes once since his momentary snooze in Carl's car on the way to the hospital the night before. Slumping onto the bed in his bare room, he promised himself at least twelve hours of sleep.

The phone woke him at nine A.M. It was Lydia Sorenson.

"I should have known you didn't skip town," she said. "Goddammit, Nashua, why didn't you give us first shot at this story?"

"What story?"

"I'm holding today's *Register* in my hand. Evan Carr's arrest is all over the front page."

"Oh. That story."

"You little prick. The publisher got hold of that note you wrote me and now he's all over my ass to explain why I convinced him to suspend you instead of sticking with the story."

"What'd you tell him?"

"I told him you were a stupid punk intern who lied to me repeatedly and refused to follow orders."

"He must be pretty angry at me then, huh?"

"I've been ordered to call you and apologize."

"Well?"

"Well what?"

"I'm waiting. Or is calling me 'you little prick' your way of saying you're sorry?"

"I'm sorry I ever met you."

"Lydia, how does it feel to know your incompetence lost the *Ledger* the biggest story to hit San Bernardino in years? And how does it feel to know you'll still be stuck in the assistant city editor's chair when your Social Security kicks in? Please, don't take that the wrong way—I'm asking as a friend."

It was the most satisfying dial tone he'd ever heard.

Nash padded out to the kitchen, poured himself a bowl of cereal, and flipped on the TV. The story was all over the news, local and network. Carr's lawyer yelling about harassment. The police fumbling to explain Klete's behavior. The FBI and the State Department denying any knowledge of a private arms deal with Venezuela. Pictures of the bunker under the Star-Time. Interviews with Homer and Escobar. The circus had come to town.

After the hottest shower he could stand, Nash returned to the hospital with an extra copy of the *Register*.

"You didn't have to put my name on the piece, too," Escobar said. "I can get bylines on my own." He began reading the front page intently. "Besides, this has all the markings of a hack job. Look at these transitions. My reputation will be ruined."

212

"You're welcome," Nash said. "And when they let you out of here, you can help me write the piece for *Esquire*."

"No shit?"

"No shit. A friend of mine at Northwestern got me the assignment. And I'm going to need your investigative skills to ferret out any federal involvement in the arms deal. That is, if you're up to it."

"No problema."

"Where's Faye? It seemed like you two had a good thing going in here yesterday."

"She's catching up on her sleep. But she promised to bring me another box of Twinkies this afternoon."

"Maybe you'd better think about cutting back on those things. I don't know if Faye would be interested in going out with the Pillsbury Dough Boy."

"Thanks for the tip, Rambler."

"Don't mention it."

Epilogue

A procession of nearly five hundred Hell's Angels lined up in two columns behind the black hearse that carried Henry Painter's body. Sandwiched between the hearse and the mile-long string of Harleys was a sedan carrying Painter's wife, his two teenaged children, and his older brother.

As the motorcade left the mortuary on Highland Avenue and made its way toward Green Acres Memorial Park in Bloomington, gawkers and plainclothes policemen with cameras and walkie-talkies clogged the sides of the expressway. Nash, riding double with a nearly recovered Homer at the back of the pack, noticed that some of the bikers were waving at the cops and swigging from bottles of beer. But the majority of Angels rolled solemnly down the road, eyes forward, denim jackets flapping in the dry breeze.

Three dozen wreaths ringed the open casket, which was draped with a red, white, and blue "Hell's Angels Berdoo" banner. None of the bullet holes in Henry Painter's body were visible.

After a non-denominational pastor spoke a few words to open the graveside service, the leader of the Berdoo Angels stepped up to deliver the eulogy. He recounted Henry Painter's heroic efforts to rescue Nash from the bunker beneath the Star-Time. And then, no longer able to control his tears, the head Angel gave his condolences to Painter's family and bowed his head in prayer.

Connie Painter, her brother-in-law, and two sons stood by the grave dressed in Sunday black. Surrounded by a sea of blue denim, they looked like the hub of a giant wheel, Nash thought. As the chapter leader raised his head, ending the moment of silence, Connie Painter turned to face the assembled crowd.

A demure, slight woman of forty-five with pretty hazel eyes, she should have appeared out of place in the ragged throng of bikers. But, like a pearl in the mouth of an oyster, she somehow seemed to fit right in, standing there between her sons, holding tightly onto their hands. As she spoke, Connie Painter calmly searched the crowd for friendly faces and nodded when she found them.

"When Henry and I joined the Berdoo Angels in the eighties, the chapter was already more than twenty years old," she said. "We didn't know it then, but we were joining a family. One of the most stable families you could ever hope to find.

"I know that all of you here today, like me and Henry, have been involved in your share of scrapes and bare-knuckle brawls at Angels rallies and biker bars over the years, and I know that some of those fights have left behind widows like me to pick up the pieces. But I also know that each chapter has stuck together through those same years, and that every member has always been ready to lay it on the line for a buddy, if and when the time came.

"Well, Henry's time came last week. He died to save one of our chapter's newest members, who was himself trying to rescue a friend from a bunch of gun-running thieves. Knowing this, I come here today not in the name of anger, but in the name of pride. I'm proud of Henry for standing up for what he believed in and for refusing to back down from a fight when the odds were against him. And I'm also proud of you for turning out to share in my grief and in the grief of my sons. You have been our family for a long time now and I wouldn't trade you for anything in the world. Thank you."

Tears touched the faces of many onlookers as Connie leaned over to give her husband a final kiss before the casket was lowered into the grave. Nash wanted to walk up to Connie Painter and thank her for sacrificing her husband so that he could live, but by the time he reached the headstone, her sons had already helped her back into the sedan.

Nash followed Homer back to his chopper. Soon they were cruising down the expressway to Indio along with the rest of the Berdoo Angels.

"Where to?" Nash yelled over the roar of the engines.

"It's time to wake the dead," Homer replied.

The name of the bar was O'Tool's. The tar-papered walls were covered, fittingly enough, with tool calendars in which scantily clad women were getting to know their torque wrenches better. Crunching through peanut shells, sawdust, and broken glass, Nash made his way to the stainless-steel bar and grabbed a cold beer from a washtub full of ice. As Jimi Hendrix's "Manic Depression" began ripping through the shack like a tornado, about a dozen Angels and their biker chicks started grooving to the beat.

"This is how I want to go out," Homer hollered.

Just as Nash started to reply, one of the Angels drove his chopper through the front door at full throttle, his long black hair flying behind him like pirate colors. As he crossed the threshold, the man yanked the handlebars hard to the left and dove headfirst onto the dance floor, sending the bike on a sideways power slide into the bar.

A series of war whoops momentarily drowned out the music when the biker stood up, dusted himself off and raised his arms in victory before grabbing a beer and heading back outside. The bike continued to idle against the bar.

"Hey, man, did you say something?" Homer yelled.

Nash shook his head. The time for rational thought was over. He downed the rest of his beer, walked over to the bar and straddled the bike. The engine felt powerful between his knees. As he pointed the chopper toward the front door, an Angel in a fur headband gave him a thumb's up.

With one hard twist on the throttle, the bike burst into the neon twilight of the Los Angeles basin and Nash found himself cruising the hard blacktop of a highway leading straight into the desert.

He was running just to feel the wind.

About the Author

Frank Sennett, author of the smash debout novel *Nash, Rambler*, has worn many hats in his career. Upon graduating from Northwestern University's Medill School of Journalism, Frank Sennett went on to receive his MFA in creative writing from the University of Montana. After serving for three years as managing editor of the Chicago weekly *Newcity*, where he earned two Chicago Headline Club awards for reporting and writing excellence, Frank beccame editor of Newcity.com, an alternive-press network. He also hosts a public radio show called *The Alternative Source*, teaches writing for the UCLA Extension and regularly writes for national magazines.

The employees of Five Star hope you have enjoyed this book. All our books are made to last. Other Five Star books are available at your library, through selected bookstores, or directly from us.

For information about titles, please call:

(800) 223-1244

or visit our Web site at:

www.gale.com/fivestar

To share your comments, please write:

Publisher
Five Star
295 Kennedy Memorial Drive
Waterville, ME 04901